LADY BETH

CAROLINE E. FARRELL

The white noise fills my head
The sound of sleepless nights
Of helpless love; and grinding teeth…

LADY BETH

ISBN: 1533698597
ISBN 13: 9781533698599

Published by NINNYHAMMER

Also by the Author

Fiction
ARKYNE, STORY OF A VAMPIRE

Film
ADAM (2013)
IN RIBBONS (2015)

JESSE

Thank fuck it's Friday. Jesse shivered as the cold river breeze bellowed up and over the central spine of Dublin city, cacophonous traffic spewing fumes and fuss, flanked by peeling billboards and neglected façades not yet sanitised by dusk and beyond. Walled quays, grey as the leaden water they bordered, merged with intersecting bridges, all linear assemblies that heaved with breathing footfall; large and loud, small and silent, a physical mass of movement and sound, disgruntled, determined, disruptive, distracted.

And watching in his stillness, half-hidden in a doorway that gave him a clear view of the bus stop at the edge of the wide footpath, Jesse observed the moving babble. Clean-cut beneath his dark manicured beard and immaculately pressed school uniform – grey pants and crisp white collar – he shuddered against another slice of icy wind. He had forgotten his blazer again, accidentally on purpose. It was bad enough that he had to wear the fucking tie, the symbol of snobbery that, except for the cack-headed prefects and the swots, no other student bothered with these days. An overpriced piece of crap that his mam insisted on replacing each time he lost one. He couldn't count how many stupid arguments he'd had with her on the subject. Her view on it: Jesse should feel proud to wear such a prestigious emblem, to signal his connection to such an educated tribe of the future. His view on it: an outdated, ridiculous emblem of class divide for the boring spawn of capitalist hierarchy, a bunch of saps that Jesse would not be caught dead hanging out with, now or ever.

Tribe? Tribe is family, blood or not, what you are drawn to, who you are drawn to. And Jesse wasn't feeling the love at school, despite his mam's obvious sacrifices for what she believed was the best education she could provide for him. He did not belong there – had never fitted in – and the uniform just added fuel to his sense of difference; a symbolic lie.

Still, there was no point in arguing with her any more. He was sick of hearing about the cost, the pride, the prestige, the opportunity, the future, and so on and on; hence the forgetting-on-purpose. He would rather freeze his butt off, *sans* blazer, since wearing a substitute jacket would result in suspension from classes – again, and the thought of facing his mam's disappointed wails was too excruciating for him to risk a repeat.

So be it. Exams would be coming soon anyway, so not long to go before he would be able to ditch this snob fuckery once and for all. Jesse knew he would do well in his leaving cert exam. He had always been lucky at tests; must have got his brains from his paternal side. Well, that wasn't entirely fair. His mam could hold her own in the grey cells department. She always did well at stuff when she put her mind to it, and even though she nagged him to study, she would sometimes admit that he got by with very little effort. A gift, apparently.

So college courses were now being considered. Law was her number one choice, but she wasn't the one who'd have to put the work in, though he suspected that short of sitting the fucking exams for him she would probably give it a go. *Whatever it takes.*

It was one thing to memorise enough poxy, useless facts and figures to get credible marks and get the hell out of school, but he wasn't sure he was ready for the serious commitment that college study would entail. And at seventeen who the hell knew what they wanted to do with the rest of their lives anyway? Seriously, what was so wrong with a gap year?

No, she said, that would be a waste, a distraction, an excuse to be lazy. Just like the transition year. *You're too smart for that, Jesse.* Trips to museums could happen on weekends, and flirting with drama and art wouldn't help him get ahead of the game. Academia would. Hard work would. Moving forward would.

Moving forward. Shit speak.

The injustice still seethed in his belly. She was so pushy, if pushy was enough of a word to describe it. He was living his life on her terms, her way, and because of it he'd begun to experience those fleeting moments when he thought he might actually hate her. She was investing far too much energy in him, every decision about his life up for debate and barely any time for her own stuff at all. It was becoming unbearable.

To say that his mam's life was boring would be an understatement – if you could call it a life at all. From bed to work, work to bed, and nothing much going on in between – except Jesse.

When he was younger it didn't seem to matter. In fact, it was quite something to be so central to her happiness. He was used to the fuss she made of him. He never went to his mates' houses; they always came to his, prompted by his mam's need to know where he was and who he was with at all times. His friends never seemed to mind – his mam was young and cool and that was deadly to them. She *was* young too. And pretty, he supposed, underneath all that blousy blandness. There was only sixteen years between them. Lots of people thought she was his older sister. Cool when you're ten. But not now.

Now it just embarrassed the fuck out of him. Now almost everything she said or did seemed to irritate him. The way she dressed: like a fucking nun; the way she ate: like a fucking bird; the way she smelled: fucking cheap. Sometimes he felt guilty about thinking of her like that, other times not, though he worried a bit, especially late at night, when he could hear her moving about the house, fidgeting, cleaning, never able to sleep.

Don't mind me, the worry-wart: her mantra when he was young and curious enough to hobble out of bed at three in the morning to find her sitting in the dimly lit kitchen. *The worry-wart who does all the worrying for the one she loves, so he doesn't have to.*

She would snuggle him close to her as she carried him back upstairs, and he would sleep like the dead, cocooned in her warm love and the knowledge that Mammy would take care of everything.

It was only now, now that he had his own girlfriend, that he'd begun to see his mam in a different light: she couldn't fix everything; she meddled too much; it was all a little unnatural. She had no friends, no hobbies, no fucking life. It was all about Jesse. Just him, and he needed to shake her off.

There's no law that says parents and children should be compatible. To be honest, he just didn't like her very much, but he didn't know why. And that made him feel guilty – and angry.

And it made him feel sorry – for himself and for her.

Of course, it had occurred to him that she must be lonely. Apart from his father, obviously, she'd never had a boyfriend, not as far as he was aware. Maybe a good shag was what she needed; maybe that would take her attention off *him* for a while. Jesse shuddered again, his thick, black, curly hair blowing across his dark, watchful green eyes.

Not cool, you bad fucker, not cool at all.

Shrugging the idea of it to the back of his mind, he checked his watch against the digital display at the bus stop. He would soon be legal, he reminded himself once more – able to do as he pleased. That was all that was keeping him from doing a runner right now.

The mid-afternoon traffic continued to drone and screech and honk, drowning out the chatter around him as Jesse huddled into the bus-stop shelter. The bus for home would be here any minute, yet still there was no sign of The Stump – not his real name, of course (Jesse had no idea what it was; nor had he any desire to know). The Stump was not to be friended – just pass the cash over and get the gear, cash he'd made selling off his vast collection of PS3 games. She would notice, of course – his mam – but he'd worry about that later. He had outgrown that stuff now anyway. He would tell her he donated it to the local library or a charity shop. She'd lap that shit up.

Jesse tensed slightly as the young man he was waiting for suddenly came into view, his face hidden beneath a hood, the colour of the sweatshirt washed-out and nondescript, much like the person secreted beneath it. The Stump could be anybody – just another ant in the army of the undead – Jesse knew it was him though, the way he held his right arm, slightly away from his body, the sleeve of his sweatshirt pulled down to cover his hand. And that awkward gait – comical really, that walk of his. Shifty, suspicious, watchful, he stopped fleetingly in front of Jesse, and though their eyes met no words were exchanged. The Stump reached out his right hand, the strange bandaged shape of it awkward as Jesse passed him the rolled up notes. Sliding it away, the sleeve fell down again over The Stump's hand, and Jesse shifted his concentration to the small plastic pellet he saw fall to the ground from the man's left hand.

The Stump moved away as the bus approached, and in one fell swoop Jesse scooped the pellet up, positioned himself in the surge to get on board, swiped his bus pass across the machine and took the stairs, two at a time, to the upper deck. Filling the back seat by spreading out his long legs to discourage anyone else from sitting beside him, he opened his fist. The plastic pellet, slightly smaller than those cap-suled toy surprises in children's chocolate eggs, was filled with tiny pills – green grenades. Jesse clasped the pellet tight-ly, feeling it warm up in his palm.

As the bus moved off, three bells, he leaned his head against the window, watching the throng of people below – more nameless ants scurrying about their business. They turned the corner on the bridge to the Southside and from his heightened view he spied The Stump again, moving with intention below on the street. Jesse noticed the dirt on his clothes, the way they hung from his skinny body, and he wondered again about his girlfriend's connection to such a lowlife.

Rebecca.

Even the sound of her name got Jesse going, and he would see her in less than an hour, smell her hair and the fra-grant skin on the back of her neck as she pushed her tongue into his mouth while his horny hands explored her body. Jesse felt the delicious rush course through him and let his head fall back as he breathed into the sense of pleasurable anticipation now spreading through him.

And now he had a present for her. All was good with the world.

ᚼ

Though still in possession of a grandiose façade and a prestigious address, the premises of Luke Thompson & Son Solicitors had seen better days. Housed on the third floor of a high-rent Georgian building, the solicitor's office overlooked St Stephen's Green, the rectangular lungs of the 'right' side of the city. From her desk, Beth had a pleasing view of the Green and she enjoyed watching life in all its quirky formations, a silent comedy; when she could relax enough to care.

The interior of the office was a sorry state: buttercream walls and ancient bare floorboards that sprung noisily underfoot, a draughty fireplace echoing whistles and moans through the spine of the building, and no longer fit for purpose. And she never could get used to the lingering food smells that wafted up from the basement-level French bistro below. Emile's, packed to capacity every night with a clientele she had to jostle past on her way home, her day coming to an end as theirs was just beginning. Comfortably off diners, the majority of them early retirees – grey-gappers – and dappled with a chatter of well-dressed hipsters rushing into the weekend to spend what they had earned. No point in them caring, she supposed; no point in them planning ahead when they didn't trust the politicians and couldn't see the benefit of saving up for a future that the generation before them had made a mess of. They would probably never earn as much as their parents did; they would probably never own their own homes. If they were lucky, they might keep their jobs. The die was cast for them all, so why would they care.

Beth couldn't help but envy their indifference.

She wished she could care less too. If she were alone in the world, she liked to think she would be brave enough to get off the grid. To get right out of the system, out to the periphery, people-watching at leisure instead of the nose-to-the-window, slave-to-routine worker bee. Clocking in and out to the uninvited reek of Emile's meaty delights, more than a tad unpleasant for her, being a committed vegetarian.

Opening the stiff sash windows didn't help either. The din from the busy quarter below would rush in – not exactly helpful when transcribing the text of a legally binding document. So Beth kept the windows shut, suffering in silence the stench, which lingered in her nostrils long after she had left the building, of overpriced cuisine that even if she were inclined to sample it she could never afford.

Not that she wasn't given ample opportunity. She had an open invitation to the regular work 'dos' that always began there, mostly to celebrate some case the company had won, or some big cheque that had come in, and bonuses in the form of food-a-plenty were the order of the day.

Luke Thompson was good that way. Always a fair boss and a hard worker himself, he had inherited the business from his father. Beth could sense him now, watching her as she carried on with her work, concentrating on the task in hand. She always tried to be careful not to draw attention to herself, and it irked her to feel his gaze on her, though she would never let him know that.

She had worked at Thompson's now for nearly seven years, and not once had anyone seen her with her hair down, either literally or metaphorically. She kept her hair scraped back, neat and prim, and never wore make-up or flashy clothes, just body-shrouding beige or black and white.

Nevertheless, she could still turn heads; she knew it, and she hated it.

Beth was always low-key about her private life too. Apart from the bits and pieces she tossed to her boss to keep him onside, she had one golden rule: *never ask, never tell.*

Luke was moving in closer now, standing next to her.

"Don't you have something better to do than to work late again, Beth?" he said, his tone gently admonishing.

She didn't look at him. *Keep the head down.* "I'm grand, Mr Thompson. I'll only be here for another hour or so, and I'll have this done and polished for you."

"I don't doubt it, but it can wait until Monday. We're going downstairs now for a bite before drinks. Want to come – just this once?"

"No thanks," she replied pleasantly. "Honestly, I'd rather finish this."

She did look at him then – and saw the disappointment on his face. It annoyed her. Why should he care whether she came or not? How dare he care!

"Ah come on! It's Friday night, Miss Downes," he teased, the use of her surname most likely, she thought, to convey his annoyance at her referring to him as 'Mr'. Luke had often asked her to call him by his first name, but she couldn't do it.

That would erase another boundary.

"I don't mind, really. Happy to get this document finished before I head off home, and I could do with the overtime. Jesse's school fees – you know?"

She hoped that dropping in that little bit of information would be enough, that he would move on, stop drawing attention to her non-existent social life. He must have known well enough by this stage that she valued her privacy, but every now and again Luke Thompson crossed the line and she didn't like it one bit, no matter how nice a man he was.

"Well, I hope that boy appreciates all that you do for him, Beth. How lucky he is to have a mother like you."

Like me? Her stomach tightened, but her expression didn't change.

"Jesse's a good kid!" she snapped defensively, feeling stupid as soon as the words were out and the awkward silence fell between them. She had overreacted and she hated doing that.

He hovered, like he wanted to say something else, but he remained silent while she cringed inside. *Damn it. None of his business!*

"I'll lock up if you like?" she said, her tone lowered to a more pleasant octave. "You go on. Get a good table before the hungry hordes start piling in."

He took a step backwards, much to her relief, and grabbed his overcoat.

"See you Monday, so." And he was gone.

A wave of relief, tinged with regret, washed over her. Shaking it off with annoyance, she sat up, straight as a poker, and went back to the text, deftly touch-typing words that meant nothing to her but that would be grammatically correct and typo free. Clean, crisp, perfect words on a clean, white, perfect page.

Parked and idling on a shaded, leafy suburban avenue, Detective Eric Bailey watched from the dirtied window confinement of an unmarked, police car, long seen better days, the indigo blue paint job pitted and scarred from much abuse and frenetic chases. From a distance, his target of interest walked with a cumbersome gait. A purposeful gait, nonetheless. Frankie Harte looked like shit, Bailey noted, amused to see the young fella ignore the nervous, sometimes dirty, looks he got from people passing by. Some would cross the street to avoid this one. Others would gladly see him dead. And though an important little prick cog in The Poet's wheel of misery, Frankie was still the least of Bailey's problems right now. Another body had been discovered this week – another murder, it seemed, though the coroner's report hadn't yet been released – and the word had just come through that this victim was transgender and barely out of his teens. Bailey felt the burn behind his sternum, as he always did when cases such as these landed on his desk. He had seen dozens of corpses in his eleven-year career in the force – babies, emaciated, beaten, or both; shootings; stabbings; cold-blooded assassinations; battered wives; tortured pensioners; suicides. Each and every case had left an indelible stain on his already low opinion of humanity. It never got easier; it never would. The world was truly fucked.

The thought scorched at his throat now as the car chugged into gear and moved up alongside Frankie Harte, driven by Bailey's partner, Rourke, the elder. A crusty greying alcoholic with a heart condition and a retirement date in his not too distant future, killing time before time killed him. When he hit the brakes, Bailey got out, getting into Frankie's path, blocking his attempts to keep moving, flashing his badge, barking orders to stop and drop. The same old routine. He wasn't surprised when Frankie attempted to flee, clumsily leaping up a wall adjacent to the footpath. Rourke remained in the car, cynical and fatigued by this familiar scenario, while Bailey grabbed the lad effortlessly, pulled him down and pushed him roughly against the wall to pat down his torso and legs.

"Do I need to force you to drop your pants?" Bailey yelled close to Frankie's ear, pulling the young man's hoodie back to reveal a once-handsome face, ravaged now by substance abuse.

Pale and gaunt, Frankie eyeballed his captor with an icy blue stare as he reluctantly reached down the legs of his tracksuit bottoms. Tugging for a bit, he winced before producing two large, clear plastic zip-locked bags, each of which had been strapped to his legs with duct tape.

Only now did Rourke amble from the car, shaking his head at the sight of the bags bulging with compacted pellets. Breaking a pellet open, he handed it to Bailey, who let the small green pills tumble to the ground where he crushed them to a sodden powder underfoot.

"Fucking grenades, Frankie? Is this what the slime ball has you dealing now?"

The young man didn't answer. There was nothing to say. Bailey was used to that too. Playing dumb was how these kids survived – turned into sub-human beings from their stints on the streets; the walking dead, decaying day to day. There was no talking to them – no reasoning with fear; no reasoning with people who had given up.

"Get in the car, you stupid little shit! And don't make me use the handcuffs!"

⋏

Entwined in each other's hungry, gangling limbs, Jesse and Rebecca made several attempts to climb the stairs. Alone with the girl of his dreams, a polished blonde, her hair cascading over her shoulders, the ends dip-dyed in hot pink, Jesse couldn't believe his luck as they stumbled and giggled, pausing for lengthy, messy kisses along the way. His mobile phone kept vibrating on silent from inside his shirt pocket, and Jesse ignored it as he led her through his bedroom door. So much older in soul than her seventeen years, she balked at the sight of the mess of clothes and clutter – this morning's discarded underwear, socks and wet towels still strewn alongside the crumpled Liverpool Football Club duvet cover from his single, unmade bed. Rebecca pulled Jesse roughly by his shirt collar, backing out of the room. Her eyes narrowed, moss green, glassy and framed in the blackest of lashes.

"Your mother's room – it's gotta be cleaner than this!"

It was a command, not a suggestion, and any reluctance Jesse might have felt had evaporated for two reasons: Rebecca made him feel hornier than he had ever thought possible, and the grenade had kicked in.

As she pushed him playfully into his mother's beige, spotless bedroom and onto her clean, cheap threadbare duvet cover, his heart knocked painfully hard against his chest wall as she forced him onto his back and straddled him. The small empty plastic pellet slipped silently to the carpeted floor, and Jesse tasted the same tart, chalky pill residue on Rebecca's tongue while she slowly undid his shirt buttons.

His phone started buzzing again.

He groaned. "I better get that. She won't stop calling otherwise."

He rolled his eyes at the sound of his mother's voice as Rebecca sat back and whacked him with a pillow.

"Why didn't you answer before, Jesse?" his Mam whined. "I've been calling for ages!"

"I was in the shower – didn't hear the phone," he said slowly, his brain and tongue attempting to synchronise. "What's up?"

He tried not to make eye contact with Rebecca, who was arching her back, the randy tease.

His mother sighed. "The school have been on again about the arrears. I'm worried now, Jesse. I'm not sure I can cover it alongside all the other expenses."

Rebecca moved off the bed and began snooping inside the wardrobe, wrinkling her nose at the sight of his mother's sensible shoes and insipid, shapeless clothes.

"I thought you were putting in for the credit union loan," he said, trying to sound interested as he watched Rebecca move to his mother's rickety chest of drawers and pick out bundles of neatly packed, plain white knickers and bras and drop them back into the drawer, her lip curled as if they were alien and disgusting to her. Jesse mouthed for her to stop, so Rebecca moved back onto the bed and began to tease him, her hands sliding up his quivering thighs, closer and closer to his aching crotch while his mam continued rabbiting on the phone.

"I have," she said, "but they've come back and said I need a guarantor. I hate the thought of doing it, but I'm going to have to ask my boss to sign for me. Jesse … are you still there?"

Rebecca had already removed her blouse. Jesse was losing the battle.

"I told you, Mam, I don't care. I hate the kip anyway!"

As he said the words, his fingers moved to a large square sticking plaster on Rebecca's chest, tucked neatly behind the strap of her purple lace bra just above the fleshy mound of her breast. He noticed there was an identical one on the other side and gazed at them quizzically, distracted for a moment from his mother's rising anxiety. Rebecca flicked his hand away.

"Don't start with that nonsense!" his mam snapped loudly.

Rebecca silently mimicked her, pulling angry faces.

"It's only one more term, and if I don't pay, it will affect you sitting the exams!"

His mother gave a weary sigh. "I'm almost home now anyway."

Jesse jolted up from the bed. "I thought you were working late?" he said, his eyes widening to alert Rebecca.

"I was, but I met my deadline earlier than I thought I would. I got the shopping done too, so be a good man and put the kettle on, would you? And it would be great if you could help your worn out mother unload it all from the car."

Jesse hung up in a panic. Pushing Rebecca away from him, he leapt off the bed and, grabbing her blouse, urged her to put it back on and get out before his mother got back.

"Why can't I meet her?" Rebecca said sulkily, refusing to do as she was told.

Still scrambling to tidy up and smoothing out the covers on his mother's bed, Jesse heard his mother's banger of a car limp up the driveway.

"Fuck, too late! You'll have to hide in my room until I can sneak you out later," he said, shoving the pouting Rebecca into his little boy's bedroom. She tried to protest, but he silenced her with a kiss. "She's a bit stressed at the moment, Rebecca. This isn't a good time to tell her about you. I'll make it up to you later, I promise."

Rebecca yanked him by the hair, pulling it hard. "You *will* make it up to me, you fucking mammy's boy!" she hissed, before scurrying off to hide among his crap as the key turned in the door.

⚔

Frankie winced at the familiar sound, setting his already sensitive teeth on edge as the cell door screeched opened. A male screw leaned in, his burly frame filling the confined space. Coiled up in a ball on his bunk, Frankie took an age to uncurl and try to sit up. Blood was seeping from the corners of his mouth – his gums, the latest humiliation of this fucking addiction – his head buzzing with pain and his legs killing him, the circulation all fucked up.

It took some effort on his part to keep up with the screw as they walked down the corridor to the taunts and jeers of other inmates: 'Nice job on yer fingers, Stumpy! Your bollix is next!' One of them he recognised: Hammer, an ugly prick with a violent rep that befitted the nickname he'd earned after he'd bashed his own son's face in because the lad couldn't steal enough for him. A nasty bastard, shoulders and upper arms disproportionally inflated and probably pumped with ropey steroids, he deliberately bumped against Frankie, reeking dire. Frankie meekly side-stepped him as laughter reverberated behind him. A little further down the corridor he paused, drawn like a magnet to read graffiti etched into a wall of flaking, mustard coloured institutional gloss paint:

When they come at you, bow down.
Refrain from belligerence.
They come back, cast your violence coldly.
They will bow down.

The Poet, 1989.

Frankie stared at the words, paralysed by the sight of the neat script, until the screw backtracked and urged him to walk on.

⅄

The prison governor, known simply as Sir, seemed a particularly delicate man to be managing such a tough gig. Gifted with an emotional intelligence unusual in any bloke Frankie had ever known, Sir was able to maintain a level of humanity despite the overcrowding and sub-standard conditions, and he was well respected, even by the inmates. Few gave him a hard time. In fact, his patrols through the corridors, smiling and emanating positive goodwill in his neat, everyday suit and tie, was somehow comforting in the powder-keg environment where prisoners circled each other with fear and rage in equal measures.

"Mr Harte, I really hoped not to be seeing you again," Sir sighed in his countryman lilt.

Limerick, Tipperary, Kilkenny? Frankie couldn't tell the difference. Most of the screws were from outside the capital and they all sounded much the same to him. Frankie was standing before Sir's desk in an office as homely as it was possible to be in this shithole institution built over a hundred and sixty years ago. When he made no reply, Sir gestured for the obviously distressed young man to sit down. Frankie did as he was told. He had no issue with the governor, a decent skin in a world of wolves.

It was the other fella in the room that Frankie wasn't comfortable with, and he watched with suspicion as Detective Bailey, wearing trendy duds, leaned on the window ledge, looking outwards. Fitting in or standing out? Frankie wasn't quite sure. Bailey looked young enough – maybe pushing forty, athletic but not bulked out like some of the other clowns Frankie had encountered – and he didn't have that Garda bang off him. Some of them reeked of it, and none could be trusted.

"I want to go back to my cell, Sir," Frankie said, a pissed-off bravado in his tone.

"Aggression will get you nowhere, Frankie. You know that. Lighten up now, the detective just has a couple of questions for you." Sir poured some water from a jug into a white plastic cup and pushed it across the desk to Frankie. "The least you can do is hear the man out, now that we've met your request for C-Wing."

Before Frankie could make some ballsy smartass comment, Bailey cut in. "I'm not surprised you asked for solitary, Frankie."

Frankie squirmed in his chair as Bailey continued to watch out the window. He could hear the whoops of prisoners being released into the exercise yard below, knew well the hostility, the pushing, the shoving, the posturing.

"Lockdown has got to be preferable to mingling with some of those scumbags," Bailey said almost to himself. "It's like peering into hell – I can feel the menace from here."

With a sense of dread that he was being sucked into yet another scenario he couldn't control, Frankie resolved to stay quiet for now. His hand shook as he took a sip from the iced water, the liquid numbing his throat before the aftershock hit his inflamed gums.

What the fuck would this dick know about it – any of it?

Bailey moved across the office and pulled up a chair to sit opposite Frankie. "The Poet has it in for you, I hear?"

It was more of a statement than a question, which Frankie ignored while Bailey, looking towards the governor for approval, took out a pack of cigarettes. Sir nodded his consent and Bailey offered a cigarette to Frankie. The need for a smoke getting the better of him, Frankie took it and held it to his nostrils, sniffing the tobacco while waiting for Bailey to produce a lighter. The detective looked at Frankie's bandaged hand.

"Did he do that to you?" he asked, frowning.

Frankie took the light with a long, greedy drag from the smoke. "Never touched me," he replied, "and you're wasting your time here. I'm no fuckin' snitch."

"The rumours are rife, Frankie. I know he did it. And covering for him isn't going to help you. Not now, after you lost his drugs. You think he'll thank you for that?" Bailey scrutinized him. "Or are you all set to say goodbye to another little bit of your anatomy?"

Frankie glared at him. "He might let me keep breathing. That's good enough for me." Despite his attempt to sound defiant, he knew his tone of voice was telling Bailey more than he cared to reveal about his trouble. He turned to the governor. "Are you getting me on the maintenance, Sir? I'm suffering here!"

Frankie had been on the programme before – many stints, in fact – and every time he lapsed back on the heroin he was convinced it was because the substitute was actually worse. That stuff seeped into his bones, made a home for itself in every organ of his body. In for the long haul and harder to wean off. The methadone was better than nothing though, and Frankie would take any fucking thing he could get into his throbbing veins right now. Anything was better than cold turkey. Nothing at all was just too bleeding painful to endure.

"We're doing our best for you, Frankie," replied the governor. "You're not the only one in here needing it. But if you help the man I might be able to bump you up the list."

"Why are you still covering for that cunt?" Bailey cut in. "What makes that scumbag so special?"

Frankie was becoming more agitated, made worse by the constant craving for chemicals, all mixed up with starvation pains because he was too sick to eat.

"Are you fuckin' joking or what?" he snapped, his voice rising an octave. He jerked his head towards the governor. "Why don't you just ask the boss here? Poet's a legend in this kip, isn't he, Sir?"

The governor didn't look at him; he was taking notes and rubbing his eyes.

"He should be thanked for advancing the literacy levels in here," Frankie went on, "and for introducing the inmates to the B section in the dictionary! Isn't that right, Sir?"

"Behave, Frankie," was all that Sir said.

Bailey grinned. fascinated by the intelligence that he saw in the young prisoner. Got under his skin every time; the waste.

Frankie focused his gaze on the glowing tip of the cigarette, the butt stained with a smudge from his bleeding gums.

"You think if you saw your old man beat your ma to death when you were a kid that you'd be alright in the head?" he asked, "Or would you be like him, a fucked-up psycho?"

"How do you know that – about his mother?" Bailey asked eagerly.

Frankie avoided eye contact by blowing smoke rings at the ceiling. When he eventually replied his tone had darkened considerably.

"You don't need me to tell you what we are dealing with here, or what happened to The Poet to turn him. You know all that shit already."

"Every piece of the jigsaw helps me move a little closer to getting him, Frankie. You can help me with that."

Frankie shook his head, a wry smile breaking out. "I can tell you that he got twelve years for killing his own father. Turned up at the cop station with his old man's blood still under his fuckin' fingernails and handed himself in. He did his time here, right here, where he learned his trade, served his apprenticeship. Finished his degree in business and law through the Open University, smart fucker that he is. But you know all that too, don't you? And you know that nothing sticks to him, that he hasn't done any time inside since that murder charge. And that's because he made it so."

"The Poet gets what The Poet wants, yeah Frankie?"

Frankie took a deep breath. "Now you have it. I understand why he did it, though – kill his own father. What do you think?" He looked straight at the detective. "An eye for an eye?"

Bailey shrugged. "That's why we have law and order. I want this scum, Frankie. I want to put an end to the trail of carnage he leaves behind him."

For a moment, the two men locked eyes, one a wounded animal caught in the wake of that carnage, the other a reluctant witness to it.

Frankie was the one to avert his eyes first. "That's the standard copper's response. Right and wrong, black and white. But what about the civilian? Don't you ever see the grey areas?"

Bailey could feel his blood boiling again as he once again came up against this bullshit code of silence. "You hear about Collins – that kid they found with his eyes gouged out?"

Frankie's head went down. Of course he had heard.

"Then you know that The Poet was behind that murder too, don't you, Frankie? He was just a kid, like you. Posed no threat to that cunt. Think about that for a second."

"His mouth must have posed a threat," Frankie snapped back. "The poor bastard would probably still be prancing around if he'd kept it shut, and well you know it!"

Bailey leapt up. "You're looking at a very bleak future, Frankie – if you have one at all." He scribbled his telephone number onto a piece of paper and placed it on the governor's desk. "It might be worth your while to stay in touch with me – that is, if The Poet doesn't get to you first."

With that last snarky comment delivered through gritted teeth, Bailey moved out of the door, striding away as the screw moved in to take Frankie's arm and lead him out of the office.

"I'll keep the detective's number here for you, son – in case you change your mind," the governor called after him as he closed Frankie's file and tipped it on top of a very large pile of similarly well-thumbed folders.

⅄

The middle-of-the-night phone call from Beth was not quite the one that Luke Thompson had been longing to receive. Seeing her number glow on his phone at three o'clock in the morning had raised his hopes, until he heard her tone of voice and the desperation in it, enough to make him leave his warm bed and rush to a police station on the other side of town.

Luke kept his feelings for his secretary to himself. The very idea of anything happening between them was ridiculous, clichéd and, judging by her reactions to him, futile. For that reason, he got on with his life and other relationships, and tried, with only the occasional lapse, to remain professional during working hours, to respect her "business only" wishes.

However aloof she insisted on being with him, over the past seven years he had grown to adore her. He could still vividly recall the first day she started working for him. Actually, it was his late father who'd interviewed her, and he remembered how impressed Luke Thompson Senior had been with the serious young woman. With her back straight as a poker, her expression so earnest, she had told him that for reasons beyond her control she had not been able to finish school and had taken no college exams. She had come straight off a state-funded back-to-work course in business studies, so hungry for the job and the experience, and so very willing. Luke's dad had always been impressed by the triers and the fighters, and Beth was certainly of that ilk. She hadn't a clue what she was doing in those early days, but being slightly besotted with her, even then, Luke Junior had made sure she hadn't messed up on anything important.

And so she fell into her stride, becoming the reliable, steady asset to the company that she was today, always professional, always discreet; never ask, never tell.

Reasons beyond her control – how many times he'd bitten his lip to stop himself from asking her about that.

When he reached the waiting area of the police station, he found her there alone, perched uneasily on the edge of a bench, her scrubbed face paler than he had ever seen it before, her body tight and fraught with anxiety. He wanted nothing more than to embrace her, but of course he knew better. Instead, he simply nodded, mumbled some suitable words of support and went directly to the uniformed policeman hunched over a log book behind a reinforced glass screen at reception.

Luke could feel Beth's eyes boring into the back of his head as he introduced himself as Jesse's legal representative and the policeman told him of the charge of possession of illegal drugs pending against the young man, soon to be legally an adult, now sweating it out in the holding cell. His mother couldn't cover the bail.

Luke signed the papers without a second thought.

Following the policeman through a key padded door, he turned towards Beth to mouth the words *five minutes* as he entered the corridor that led to the holding cells, a short journey over worn marmoleum flooring and patterns of scuffed hand and footprints on the dented, once-white walls.

It was a good deal longer than five minutes before Luke returned to the reception area with Jesse, an insolent expression on the young man's ashen face. While Beth's questioning gaze remained glued to her son, Luke gestured for Jesse to sit down.

"Wait there, and say nothing. That shouldn't be a problem for you."

His tone was harsh, but he'd just witnessed the tough-nut impudence that emanated from the youngster and he found it surprising – shocking, in fact. Luke hadn't done much criminal law, but when he was devilling at the start of his career he had found himself in the company of some tight-lipped, canny criminals. Watching Jesse now, taking his "right to remain silent" to the extreme, and responding to all the policeman's questions with stony-faced defiance despite the threat of a prison cell, transported him back to those days. It unsettled him, not for himself but for Beth, bringing up a boy on the verge of manhood whom she obviously didn't know very well.

He tried to be tactful, but truthful just the same. "They are charging him with possession of drugs – illegal pills – amphetamines, Beth. I'm covering the bail, but he hasn't done himself any favours. He won't say where he got them from."

Luke was holding her by her elbow, could feel the full weight of her body in his supportive grip. Her eyes never left her son and Luke wondered if she was even listening to him.

"I can get him the best representation, but you're going to have to convince him to give up the dealer. They'll go easier on him if he does. First offence. Beth, listen to me." He turned her towards him. "There have been some deaths recently related to this drug. He has to say where he got them from. Do you understand?"

"Can we go now? Are we free to leave?" she asked, and Luke could feel her sense of desolation, could see the fear in her eyes.

"Yes, for now. You can take him home," he reassured her quietly. "I'll drive. We can collect your car in the morning."

Outside in the car park, Beth went towards her own car, Jesse, still silent, following. "I can drive us home myself, Luke," she told him, "You've done so much for us already. Thank you."

Luke considered protesting but changed his mind. He'd known this woman long enough to know that her pride and need for privacy took precedence. He stepped back and watched her hand tremble as she made several attempts to get the key into the ignition of her rust-bucket of a car.

Beside her, as she gave Luke a small, grateful wave before driving off, her son stared at him with the coldest look of contempt Luke had seen in a very long time – a look that chilled the bones of his spine.

⋏

In the half light of the prison cell, echoes of time standing still – a myriad of whistles, shuffles and low moans – filled the claustrophobic space. Frankie swallowed a lump in his throat, squeezing his eyes shut as he tried to erase the pictures in his head. The images that haunted his days and nights; that morning, three years ago now. The hammering on the door, the dull thuds of the shots, the growing pool of blood on the hall carpet as he cradled his father's head in his arms, and time standing still as the car screeched away and the blood seeped into his jeans as he waited a lifetime for the ambulance to arrive. And waited, with this smell in his nostrils, there still, the smell of a broken human being, bleeding out, and that sound in his ears, the wretched gasps and gurgles as his father struggled to breathe, his precious gulps of air being sucked back out through the gaping, scorched hole in his neck.

Frankie twisted and squirmed in the narrow bunk, unravelling the bandage from his hand. It took him some time to pluck up the courage to look at the stump, a scabby mutilated mess, three fingers missing. His stomach turned and he swallowed again painfully, squeezing his eyes shut and stifling his sobs under the pillow.

Muted music throbs through the walls of the storeroom, cluttered with junk and supplies. Posters peel from the walls, adverts for the burlesque show at The White Lady, the 'Come as You May' Burlesque Ball hosted by Miss Subrosa.

His face battered and bruised, Frankie struggles in vain. Two men, known to him only as Wally and Hatch, scum-dirty rough necks, pock-faced and tattooed, restrain him.

Enter The Poet, a man in his early 50s, austere, well-groomed and elegantly dressed; mobster movie cliché if he wasn't so fucking real.

Wally pulls at Frankie's arm, pushes his hand down flat onto the table. Frankie sobs as The Poet slowly leans across, his face closing in, expensive cologne lingering between them.

"You've made things too personal for my liking, Frankie," The Poet says through perfect, pearl-white veneers as the shivering Frankie attempts to plead his case. Wally silences him with a smack across the mouth, The Poet stepping backwards to avoid the snot-soaked ruby droplets that splatter on the table.

"Just like your da, eh, Frankie?" The Poet continues. "Now, about my money. How are you going to pay me back?"

Frankie chokes on a cough, abject fear squeezing air painfully from his lungs as the blood pours from his nose.

"Guess we'll just have to sort something out then, son, but in the meantime, I'll need to keep you focused."

The Poet looks towards Hatch and nods. Hatch stuffs a dirty rag into Frankie's mouth.

"I'll have one finger for every ten grand you owe me – and that'll do for now."

As The Poet leaves the room, Hatch lifts a meat cleaver and slams it down on Frankie's fingers, oblivious to the young man's muffled howls of agony.

🙠

Pacing his room, Jesse grimaced. What a fucking night. That journey home with his mam had been intense. She was close to hysterics. Talk about overreacting! At one point, he thought she was going to crash the car. He had even contemplated giving her a slap just to calm her down.

"I can't believe this!" she had wailed. "Sweet Jesus in Heaven, what have you done? Sweet fucking Jesus!"

There was no point in answering her; she would never get it. So Jesse had just stared out the passenger car window and let her rant away.

"Christ! Do you realise what a serious charge you're facing?"

Okay, he could admit now, now that he was in the privacy of his own bedroom, that he had been dismissive of her concerns, which had really freaked her out, but it was just a first offence. Jesse knew he would probably get off with probation. That's what Rebecca thought too.

He had tried to explain it to his mam, but everything he said seemed to frustrate the hell out her, and then she lashed out at him, swerving the car all over the road as she thumped him on the shoulder, spitting anger before lunging at him again, slamming his cheek with the back of her hand. Now that was a shock. His mam had never hit him before, and fuck did it hurt!

"You stupid fucking idiot!" she had screamed. He had never heard her curse before either. "You haven't a clue – not a fucking clue what you're talking about!"

Jesse had held his burning face as she drove blindly, a mad woman, and for the second time he wanted to slap her, but most of all he wanted her to shut up.

"I'm not having this! You're not throwing everything I've done for us back in my face now. We're going to have to move. We'll disappear"

He yelled at her then, demanded that she relax. *What the fuck was she on about?* Overreacting, irrational. It was a one-off thing; Jesse didn't intend doing it again.

She didn't like that – his tone, his defiance – and he instantly regretted it, for she got worse, her voice rising to an excruciating shrill.

"Don't you tell me to relax, don't you ever! And for the record, you can bet your life it was just one time, because I swear to you, Jesse Downes, I'll smother you in your sleep before I watch you fester and die a stinking, rotten junkie!"

Those words – alien, vitriolic – had scalded him and Jesse had wanted to jump from the moving car so as not to hear his own mother utter such brutal threats. But he would probably die on the road anyway, the way she was driving. She was in such a frenzy, something he had never seen before. For the first time in his life, he felt afraid, and so he had lowered his voice and attempted to calm down in the hope that she would do the same.

"I'm not that stupid. You know that I'm not."

It worked, or it appeared to as she lifted her foot off the accelerator a little and brought her shoulders down from her ears.

"That's what they all say."

She drove the rest of the way home in silence while he nursed his throbbing face. He could taste blood in his mouth; he'd bitten his tongue when she'd slapped him. He despised her for that, for the humiliation, but he chose to say no more. Instead, he took his head out of the situation, out of his mother's shitty little car, and thought about Rebecca, about the sex and the feeling of euphoria from the grenades before the cops raided her mate's apartment and all hell broke loose.

The drugs were Rebecca's, brought especially for the party, but Jesse couldn't let the cops find them on her, now could he? He was just as guilty anyway, so better him than her, for sure.

⚓

Eric Bailey was of the belief that dogs were the coolest creatures on the planet. He owned, or at least he liked to think he owned, a pair of huskies, which he'd had for four years now. Dynamo and Houdini, named for their innate ability to escape through burrowed tunnels and over fences whenever the opportunity arose. Majestic white beasts with grey-tinged saddlebacks, beautiful blue-eyed creatures that proved to be better company than friends, family or women, if Bailey's past record was anything to go by. Not that he didn't like women – he loved them – it was the shit that generally came packaged with the relationship he'd grown weary of.

He had only had three meaningful relationships in his entire adult life, none of which survived longer than two years. The last one, Susan the film producer, had even moved in with him for a while. That had been fun, sharing a love of movies, food and sleep deprivation. She hadn't minded the long hours he worked; she was often away on film sets, at premieres, or travelling to festivals and foreign locations, seeking out co-productions and funding opportunities. Her life was full and exciting without him. She didn't need to be there all the time, and she didn't need him either, which made their hook-ups even more thrilling. The perfect relationship, but for one thing: Susan couldn't get along with his dogs, and that was a deal-breaker.

And now he was forty-one and single again. That wasn't a good thing – or so his widowed mother, his married sister, his crusty work colleague and his so-called friends, most of them coupled up, kept reminding him – and inevitably followed it up with the question: *Don't you want kids?*

Fuck no! Who in their right mind would choose to bring children into this cesspit? was his usual response, even if he did feel guilty when the question came from his mother. She'd already been disappointed by his older brother, the black sheep of the family, the son she no longer mentioned by name, except when she had been on the wine, and the tears would flow.

Bailey would never admit it out loud but he did experience the occasional paternal pull in his gut, especially when he visited his younger sister Gracie's mental gaff, though the feeling came and went pretty quickly after spending time with her four boys and the potty-training deposits that didn't always reach their target, the scattered mountains of toys and dirty washing, and the sounds of 24/7 cartoon time. Every one of those kids seemed smarter than Bailey, the way they'd look at him, sizing him up, the occasional guest who'd visit them laden with sweets that his sister didn't want them to have. The slightly nervous-in-their-presence uncle, always one step behind with the latest toy craze, book or DVD. Sometimes worthy of their playtime, their questions, the novelty soon wearing off in favour of the TV and some posh pink pig, talking dogs, talking cars, talking trolls, or the antics of a cute little Russian kid in a headscarf.

And so his visits were sporadic, usually limited to birthdays and Christmas, and the guilt would surface as soon as he had made his escape. Maybe when they were older he'd be able to connect with them better; a better uncle, a better brother. Now just wasn't a good time. Bailey was too stressed out to be around kids – or family. Bad company with the stuff he carried around with him. And he couldn't get that dead kid, Collins, out of his head. The report had landed: the lad had been smothered; a punishment killing, no contest. He only hoped the kid was dead by the time his eyes had been cruelly gouged out. The killer had definitely been sending a message with that one.

A message about what, though? What did the kid know? What had he seen?

Bailey was also puzzled by other marks the autopsy had discovered: puncture wounds, like tracks on his flesh, back and front on the torso, and not caused at the time of death. A strange little detail that bothered the fuck out of Bailey. Just as well he didn't have a partner to share his life with. Or his thoughts.

Dogs win. Dogs didn't mind if he came home grumpy and silent, hitting the vodka instead of the kettle, and the takeaway instead of the kitchen. Dogs liked Chinese leftovers and were satisfied with a rough grapple around the ears by way of affection before settling, not at his feet but on his feet as he mindlessly clicked the remote control until some random pulp appeared on the telly to send him off to sleep on the couch.

And that's where he was when his mobile rang, his body stiff and cramped as he dreamt of eyeless corpses and gaping wounds, and his feet numb, trapped beneath the weight of his snoring dogs. Grasping for the phone, he answered it with all the enthusiasm of a growling bear, but soon was sitting upright when he recognised the voice.

⅄

Talking to the cops went against everything Frankie had learned from his three years on the streets. Even making this call was a risk, despite the elaborate plan Sir had set up to enable him to do it without arousing any suspicion among the inmates, some of them happy enough, or desperate enough, to kill at the whiff of a snitch.

Frankie had declared illness in the middle of the night so he could be brought down to the infirmary. He didn't have to pretend much – the tiny amounts of phy they were administering just wasn't cutting it. And he felt as sick as a dying dog when he sat in the governor's office once more, this time with a proper cup of tea in a proper mug, and was given the phone and Bailey's number.

"So you can get me out of here?" he asked the cop.

He heard the initial surprise in Bailey's voice, before his alert professionalism kicked in.

"I appreciate the call, Frankie, but I need something more substantial than a rehashed biography of the fucker!"

"You'll get what you need, but not until I'm out – and you know I've fuck all to lose." Frankie waited, hoping the anxiety he was gulping down with his tea wasn't evident at the other end of the phone.

"Might take a while. I can't get you a safe house overnight," Bailey replied.

Frankie wasn't worried about that. "One poxy lock down to another? No thanks. I'll take my chances on the streets."

"Can't allow that, Frankie. You'll be marked the minute you're outside those gates. I don't need another butchered corpse on my books."

Frankie's agitation got the better of him. "You don't get it, do you? I have to get out of here now! The Poet likes to make an example of fuck-ups like me. In here he's the devil – no, he's fuckin' god! I'd be dead already only he's enjoying this. A butchered corpse is what I'll be a lot quicker if I have to stay in here!" He grimaced at his mutilated hand. "Kind of money we're talking about doesn't make a dent in him, but he can't let anyone, especially small fry like me, slip through. Bad for business, bad for his rep."

A silence fell between them on the line, the only sound Frankie's quickened breathing.

"I have to ask you Frankie," Bailey said eventually, "how did you end up in this mess. You don't exactly come across as a—"

"A brain-dead stoner?" Frankie cut him off. "You're a bit soft for a razzer, you know that? Doesn't matter what you've come from, drugs fuck us all up – simple! Now look, I can help you. You know it, so get me out and you'll get what you want, you have my word, alright?"

He didn't wait for Bailey's reply before hanging up. The pain is his legs was getting worse, and he was finding it difficult to breathe. He needed to lie down, to be in the dark. He needed to sleep.

⅄

Jesse waited for Rebecca to text him back. She'd sent him a half-naked photo of herself, lips puckered to a pout, full of the possibilities, her hands strategically placed over her bare breasts, with a message: *Where UR hands should be right now!*

He'd sent her back a question: *What are those plasters on your chest all about?*

They'd already been communicating half the night. She was glad he was okay. He was glad she was okay too. He wasn't worried about the cops and neither should she be. He wouldn't be giving them anything. He wasn't a snitch, or a fucking idiot, despite what his mother thought.

His mam, sobbing loudly for hours now, non-stop, and despite Rebecca's assurance that she would get over the shock, it bothered Jesse that she was taking it so badly. He did appreciate everything she had done for him over the years, he really did, and he would try to make it up to her. With his texting conversation with Rebecca still open on his silenced phone, he went to his mam's room, equal measures of pity and annoyance engulfing him as he saw her curled up on her bed.

"It *was* the only time, I swear," he said quietly. "And it's not going to happen again."

That seemed to perk her up, which was a relief to him, until she did that thing – lifted back the duvet for him to get in. Jesse used to like that when he was a kid and couldn't sleep. But now, it just felt so wrong. Yet if it meant keeping her sweet, what the hell. He climbed in beside her, still wearing all his clothes, still clutching his phone, eagerly awaiting Rebecca's next message, and lay on his back, just him and his mother, staring at the familiar intricate pattern of shadows cast on the ceiling by the plastic shade of the landing light. It seemed like a lifetime ago now that he used to clamber in here late at night and she would cuddle him close, all warm and safe, while they made up stories about the shadow patterns. He'd fall asleep with images of friendly ghosts and unicorns in his head, dreaming of adventures that led from his mam's magic ceiling light to mystical landscapes made of chocolate. He'd always find a sweet surprise under his pillow the following morning, and for a time, he really did believe in the magic, and all those little things that were once so special between them.

"I still don't understand, Jesse. Why? What's going on with you that you'd want to do drugs? You have a good life. I take care of you, don't I?"

There was so much anguish coming off her, as if someone had died, like it was all about her, and he felt his irritation rise again.

"Look, I messed up, let you down, and I'm sorry for that. But everybody does drugs these days. It doesn't mean you get addicted or anything stupid like that. It was just for the party, for the buzz. It's not like I'm a junkie, or an alcoholic or anything!" Without looking at her, he could feel her scrutinising him, that burning, searching stare of hers, but he kept his gaze on the ceiling. "You weren't serious about moving, were you? A bit extreme, don't you think?"

That bit of what she had said earlier had been bothering him. His life was just getting good now that he had Rebecca, and school was almost out. He wasn't prepared to give it all up just to appease his overprotective mother's anxiety.

"Where did you get the stuff from?" she asked.

He'd been waiting for this question, but there wasn't a hope in hell of him telling her, so he just ignored it. "You'll be going on your own if you're thinking of moving, Mam. I won't be going with you."

She sat up then and turned on the light. The ceiling suddenly became glaringly white, the shadow magic dead and gone, and he was forced to look her in the face, meet her eyes, red-rimmed from crying. No, Jesse's heartstrings just weren't being tugged. He'd noticed it before, though he'd never said anything, but now when he looked at her, really looked at her, he realised he had nothing in common at all for this intense, controlling woman.

"If we tell the police where you got the drugs this could all go away," she suggested. "So tell me now, Jesse, where did you get them?"

Was she crazy, too? There was no way he was telling the cops anything!

He was hardly in a position not to, she argued. He'd been caught red-handed in possession of two hundred euros worth of illegal amphetamines – the street value was five times more – money that didn't come out of his pocket.

Jesse was a little taken aback, maybe even amused, that she seemed so knowledgeable about drugs. Strange thing it was to hear his mother talk about the street value of anything, like she really knew what the fuck she was on about. She wasn't giving up either, and now she was yelling again.

"Who gave them to you, Jesse? You have to tell me!"

He slipped up then, almost said Rebecca's name, but he clammed up just in time. She was on to him though; she'd always had a knack for reading his face.

"Jesse, who are you covering for?"

His phone was flashing now. Rebecca again, with another message and another mouth-watering photograph. He sat on the edge of the bed, turning away from his mam, and read the text: *You want to know wot the marks are? Come get me – now!*

Even with his back to her he could feel his mam's eyes piercing him, the brewed tension between them. And then she grabbed him, her spindly fingers digging into his flesh, a vice-like grip around his arm.

"Just drop it, okay!" he yelled, desperate to shrug her off. "I said it was a one off. There'll be no more trouble. And don't listen to that idiot boss of yours – I'll get off this time. I'm not concerned, so don't you be either!"

But she just couldn't let it go. "We don't have secrets from each other, Jesse. We shouldn't!"

That was priceless, coming from her. Jesse's blood ran cold as he turned to look at her, a dark grimace clouding his handsome face. As he stood up she clung onto his arm. Contempt for her washed over him; he couldn't help it.

"You hear yourself, Mother? You hear what you just said?"

He spat the words out, knowing at once that he had her beaten. She retreated, physically and emotionally. How small and powerless she seemed now as he looked down on her, until she came back at him, a terrier, yapping behind him as he attempted to leave the room.

"So you met a girl and she gave you drugs, just like that, and now you're covering for her. Is that it?"

Her tone made his blood boil again. She was changing the subject, turning things around, and yes, she'd hit a nerve.

"No! Not just like that, but what the fuck would you know!"

She recoiled, obviously shocked by his hostility, pleading with him to stay calm; they could talk this through. She reached her hand out to him but he smacked it away and turned his back on her, defiance itching away at him.

"Not that it's any of your business, but yeah, I am seeing someone – and I'm crazy about her. In fact, I think I love her. So fucking what?"

He could almost see the shock exhale from her, deflate her, and it felt good, satisfying, until yet again, she bounced back, her condescension adding insult to injury.

"Don't be ridiculous!" she snapped, "You're only seventeen!"

That pissed him off even more, coming from her. So he asked her. Had she loved Jesse's father when she fucked him? Fucked him when she was only fifteen? Man, the look on her face.

And then she ran, out of the room and into the bathroom, locking the door. Locking him out.

We shouldn't have secrets between us. She always said that. Fucking hypocrite with her fake bullshit! He followed her, angrily thumping on the door.

"Since we're sharing now, why don't you tell me who my father is? It's my right to know, after all. No secrets, right?"

When she didn't answer, the rage inside him soared and he kicked the door.

"Mam!"

Still she made no reply. Her silence infuriated him. He pounded his fist into the wall at the side of the bathroom door, smashing through the plaster and leaving a gaping hole there as the urge to hurt her raged through him.

And he ran, downstairs and out of the house, away from her – the liar, the faker.

Ghost Child

Rebecca woke up with a start, sweating, clammy and nursing the same dull headache she'd had for a week. Coming down from a bad trip and dreaming of Jesse again, she replayed the events of that night in her mind: the sea of bodies at the club as it surged and pulsated in time to the music as she watched him scanning the floor, looking for her, seeing her, wanting her. She'd ignored him on purpose; it was all part of the game, her body throbbing in sync with the beat, knowing she was being watched – and not just by him. When he came towards her, she willed him to be masterful, to claim her as his own. How she had loved that! And she'd leapt into his arms, her legs straddling his waist while he'd gripped her tightly, spinning her around and around, smiling ecstatically. Not a care in the world. Not a care. And as she slipped the packet of grenades into his back pocket, all pretty shades of mint green and citrus yellow, she kissed him passionately, hungrily, wanting him tonight, wanting him now. Knowing that he craved her just as badly, knowing that he would do anything to have her. No words necessary, it was all in the smile, in the touch. It was all in the eyes.

She had watched him shuffle away from her, disappearing into the throng of the dance floor, and while he did his business in the men's room, she rocked out, moving her body-con bandaged figure suggestively as the boys looked on, wanting her, and the girls looked on, envying her. And as she flirted with her hungry eyes, she imagined him swallowing her little gifts, and how he would soon feel exactly like she did right now, so fucking powerful, so alive, and the night was only beginning.

She had one more surprise for him, had been leading up to it, slowly, slowly, telling him just what he needed to know in the moment. Soon it would be time for the reveal; saving the best for last.

It wasn't long before he was back. She had watched him stagger towards her. She'd felt funny inside; everything was distorted – colours, movement, laughing faces. Perspiration tickled her hairline and beaded on her upper lip, her make-up wrecked, the stain of her ruby lips smeared across her cheeks as she wiped her burning hot mouth. Her tongue had felt bigger than it should, invading the too-small space of her mouth, and her throat was dry. She scrutinised Jesse as he came towards her. He looked weird. He was sweating profusely, a giant sponge, and he was bumping into everyone and getting pushed back and around. She'd tried to call out to him, but her tongue just wouldn't co-operate.

And then she froze – as everything around Jesse froze – and she watched his legs turn to water and buckle beneath him, his body crashing down hard.

She watched the crowd surge in on him, an ebbing wave of noise and mayhem as they recoiled, clearing a space as he jerked and convulsed on the dance floor. Blood spurting from his nose, Jesse looked at her, his eyes bulging, pleading.

She didn't like it. She didn't like it one bit, and as people leaned in towards him, shrieks of panic with hands pulling at Jesse, yelling at him, screaming for help, she had withdrawn from the horror of it all, blending invisibly into the chaos.

This time it suited her very well not to be the centre of attention.

⋏

If she had been able to cry, Beth's tears would have cut as bitter and smiting as the rain that spilled down on the gathering of mourners she was standing apart from, a careful, protected distance between her and the rest of the world, as always. She watched them, damp and shivering, all huddled around the grave of her son, micro groups of near strangers, straining to hear the prayers that emanated from a priest she did not even know. Solemn, though his words were rushed as the deluge grew in strength and din, the priest went through the motions of what surely must be a weekly, if not a more frequent morbid ritual.

She wondered if the holy man, or indeed, any of them, was imagining as she was, seeing what she saw; her son's beautiful body, not yet fully blossomed to manhood, and already beginning to stink and rot. The child she bore, reduced to nothing more than food for devouring maggots, there it lay, alone, not more than six feet from their sodden shoes.

Where had he gone. And how would she follow him?

A scattering of teenagers in school uniforms were watching her, skinny boys in oversized grey jumpers, and womanly girls, their make-up and hairstyles defying school rules. Shocked and awkward in equal measure, they knew neither how to react nor what to say. Later, she imagined, they would congregate somewhere else – a parent-free zone – unified by their reactions to the death of one of their own, hugging each other, crying, tweeting, Snapchatting, paying tribute to their friend on his Facebook page. His *public profile,* another thing she never knew he had until the day after his death when she went into his room, seeking out the essence of him. Needing to smell his lingering presence, on the sheets, on his clothes, in the hairs of his comb – before it faded forever. Touching the things that he owned, the cabinet drawers full of long forgotten gadgets and useless copper coins that he regularly discarded from his pockets; playing cards, keyrings, watches, socks, all from her, the expensive aftershave she bought him for Christmas, still in the gift bag. She'd run her fingertips across the keyboard of his computer to sense his touch, looking for traces of where his fingers had been – should still be – a residue that might connect her to him, and there it was, a world he kept from her. His social media page opened up, and though she couldn't access it, she could see the photograph, and Beth reeled from the sight of it: her son's arms wrapped around *that* girl with the pink dip-dyed head, bare, tanned shoulders and painted-on slugs for eyebrows; her beautiful boy nothing more than a handsome accessory for *that* girl to wear like a trophy as she pouted for their "selfie".

Beth had also found a sentence scrawled on his bedroom wall in lipstick: *I'll get to fuck you yet! Love, R.* And the knickers, *that* girl's, Beth supposed, under his pillow, hearts and kisses written in indelible ink: *For when I'm not with you.*

Condoms too, dear god! How did she not know?

There were other photographs on his Facebook page; Jesse Downes, tagged. Posted by his friends, she guessed, though she did not recognise any of them; kids with better mothers than she had been, with caring fathers, attentive and present and setting good examples. Clued-in parents who did their job properly, knowing exactly how and where their teens spent their leisure time – instead of assuming – instead of being so smug. Parents who were at this minute learning from her nightmare, taking nothing for granted, doing the research and being extra vigilant. To know the score, for they also knew that Jesse's death, a death in youth and what lay beyond it, would fascinate these youngster's fertile imaginations as much as it would scare them. And for a short while, even in their alone time, each one of them would be hit hard by the realisation that Jesse wasn't coming back, ever.

See you on the other side.

This wasn't supposed to happen, invincibility was not a given; a sobering thought for the young to ponder when life seemed to stretch ahead with such infinity.

Don't end up like Jesse Downes.

Her son had taught them a valuable lesson, and there they all were at the funeral, staring at her, his poor, dopey excuse of a mother, shocked and devastated, dry-eyed, haunted, soaked to the skin as the rain poured down.

Crying had never been an option for Beth, not then, not now, not ever, and so, she held her face up, chin out in fake defiance against the pain that encompassed her and the grief that screamed inside.

Luke Thompson was there, standing behind her, watching attentively as the funeral ended and the people began to disperse. She would let him help her – this time. There would be no family gathering, there was no family. No pub grub, no soup and sandwich reception. There would be nothing. Beth would not allow it. In his short life, there had only ever been the two of them, and in his death, it would be no different.

Then Beth spotted her – *that* girl, the pink-blonde in the profile pic with her head tilted so covetously into the crook of Jesse's neck. The one so arrogant to leave her crude writing on the wall, the one who Jesse had chosen above her, his mother.

Standing alone and at a distance, the girl could have been Jesse's age, though she looked older. Prim and polished in her maroon school uniform, the mark of another good school, and Beth would know. The girl was staring across at her; the last person to see Jesse alive, and Beth moved quickly, breathless as she charged forward, oblivious to her own arresting, manic state, her dark hair plastered to her head, her shapeless coat covering her petite frame as the rain-soaked hem lapped heavily at her ankles.

The girl ran away before Beth could reach her, and although she wanted more than anything to pursue her, to get a hold on the one person who might give her the answers she craved, her body failed her and she felt her energy sag in defeat. She was old now, older than any age as gentle arms enfolded her, stopping her in her tracks, supporting her weight, and though she tried to break free, she could not find the strength. Becoming his mother was to know that she was dying, closer to her grave every day that he grew stronger. And that was okay. But not this. This was not okay, this terrible, cruel trickery, and Beth wanted to follow him, her boy, to fall and to keep falling; to hold him in the darkness.

She sank to her knees, helpless, her aching flesh and bones heavy and cumbersome as those same gentle arms lifted her from the dirt. Luke's arms, changing her course, moving her past the group of young people, a beautiful army of grey and maroon, staring at her as she was lead out towards the cemetery gates.

One young man stood out from the rest – Darren, the only one who Beth knew. He was a nice kid, a community college kid, a solid boy from a solid family, his expression betraying how deeply he was feeling Jesse's death. Beth reached out to him, her hands streaked with dirt, and, visibly upset, Darren stood still and allowed her to hug him. She held on to him, too long for comfort, and his body slackened a little as he clumsily let his arms dangle by his sides. She fumbled to straighten his school tie and he let her.

"I can still see the two of you, barely into your teens, bounding up the road together, and always, always full of mischief," Her voice small and choked, she paused, recalling the stress of that move back to Dublin, almost six years ago, and how difficult it had been to convince Jesse that it was the best thing for him. She had assured him that he would make new friends, that everything would be fine, but it wasn't, not at all, not until Darren had come on the scene and Jesse, relieved to have found a buddy, began to relax. "Here comes trouble, I'd sing."

Here comes trouble.

She lost the thread of her thought to a distant time; a life that had been blissful. And now she was sliding again; the world turning upside down, the mud grazing her cheek as she hit the ground, hard. He was at her side again, Luke, hauling her to her feet, wiping the dirt from her face and her hair as Beth tried to shake him off, a crazed look in her eyes as tiny, peppered beads of blood bubbled over the taut flesh on the bone of her cheek. She grabbed Darren's arm and held it tight, drilling him with questioning eyes as he struggled with his emotions.

"You should talk to Rebecca. Ask her! Ask her why this happened!" he said, sensing exactly what it was Beth wanted to know.

Darren pulled away then, angrily wiping his eyes with his sleeve as he ran off.

⋏

Some people are just born good, and they stay that way until they die. Luke Thompson is of that kind, always knowing the right thing to do – in this case, bringing her home to run her a hot bath so she can wash the cold and the mud and the blood from her body. But never the scars. He gently cleans and unpicks the dirty gravel from the scrapes on her cheek too – though she doesn't feel a thing – and he offers her tea and something to eat. Toast, though she won't remember eating it.

But *I* relish it all.

The smell, that lovely, comfort of melted butter on hot bread as all the while, she chews, barely seeing him. And he turns down the duvet on her cold bed and folds her into it so that she can bury herself beneath its weight. And while she sinks to the depths of her dreams, the lurid, dark visions of another life, he waits in the quiet stillness of the night. Sitting at her chipped, second-hand kitchen table, distraught at the grief she is suffering, and he wishes that none of this had happened, that she didn't have to suffer like this; and he wishes that he could have her.

But in the morning, her tear ducts still dry as a bone; her eyes will be slow to open, but when they do, they will be all-seeing, all-searching, and filled with a grit that will never go away.

⅄

Rebecca still wasn't sleeping well, and no wonder. That business with Jesse had really scared her. If her parents ever found out – Jesus, she could hardly bear to think about the consequences. And that cunt of a woman knew where she lived now. How fucking dare she bring that shit to her door! Imagine if her father had been home, or if her lush of a mother had answered the door. Life at home was sketchy enough, what with keeping Pops happy, when he was around, and subduing Mammy with her favourite gin and prescription antidepressants.

Some days, like today, Mammy didn't even get out of bed. It didn't bother Rebecca anymore. Nothing did, except maybe when Pops came home from his latest business trip and the arguments would start again before his bag was even unpacked. Hushed hostile voices behind their bedroom door, sniping sarcastic tit-for-tat insults at each other until it got out of hand and however muted he attempted to keep it, through gritted teeth, her father's hatred seeped through the walls like poison.

Not in front of Rebecca.

Well fuck that! Not that she disagreed with what he had to say – her mother was a lazy wagon. Rebecca could barely stand to be in the same room as her. She often wondered why they stayed married when they obviously hated each other's guts. She asked her mother once, if she didn't love him, and didn't care enough some days to get up and wash herself, why did she bother at all? Why stay?

Why don't you divorce us?

She never got an answer, which drove her insane as her mother retreated every time behind the locked door of her bedroom, curtains drawn, under the duvet, a sniffling; sad clown.

Sorry for hurting your fucking feelings? Fuck that too!

Rebecca had asked Pops why *he* stayed, but only once, for he had given her an answer that she still cherished: he would never leave her, his daughter. Rebecca was his life, his future, and for that reason alone he would never leave the woman who had given birth to her. To break up the family would be to hurt Rebecca, and to hurt Rebecca would be the death of him.

A father has responsibilities.

He *was* a good, if absent, father. Strict and proper, and although he never got angry with her, she knew it was always there, that short fuse, under the surface. She recognised it. Like daddy, like daughter, she got it: that simmering unhappiness making them sullen and short-tempered, always ready to blow.

It had been a blessing that her mother was in one of her drunken slumbers today when Jesse's mother called. Rebecca felt sorry for Mrs Downes – of course she did. She had been really fond of Jesse and had some good times with him. But for fuck's sake, he'd taken that stuff of his own free will. And he was greedy with it. Nothing to do with Rebecca, really.

The woman's haunted face though, and her flat emotionless tone as she'd stood on the doorstep way too close for comfort. Fuck, she gave Rebecca the creeps. She was looking for someone to blame, wasting no time getting stuck in with the questions: who gave her son that poison? Who put those pills into his hand?

Rebecca swore on her own mother's life that she didn't know.

That's what she'd also told the cops when they came to her school to question Jesse's friends. They weren't a patch on Mrs Downey though – wiry little Rottweiler, persistent and suspicious, firing question after question, all of which Rebecca had responded to by snapping back, *How would I know?*

Until that last dig. Mrs Downes wanted to know why her son's best friend had told her to talk to Rebecca. Now that had rattled her. What the fuck had Darren said?

She'd clammed up then, but as she'd tried to close the front door, Jesse's mother pushed against it, her foot in the gap, threatening to tell Rebecca's parents. That was worrying. Rebecca didn't like to be worried. It made her anxious, and there was only one way to deal with anxiety. Her wounds were healing nicely from the last time, the scabs deliciously itchy, tingling, and that lovely rush of longing was building up inside her for the next time. She would have to sort that out, and soon. Nothing could get in the way of that.

So Rebecca had put on her best face – the little-girl-that-could-do-no-wrong face that always worked on Pops. Creased up with worry, she'd pleaded with Jesse's mother not to get her into trouble; she'd explained how upset her parents would be and how frightened she was of disappointing them. They were strict, she'd told her, scary, violently strict. Mrs Downes had promised to leave her alone if she would give her a name. So once Jesse's mam swore never to say who had told her and never to come back, Rebecca gave her a fucking name.

Frankie. Some people called him The Stump and Jesse's mother would know why when she saw him. Mrs Downes wasn't finished with her questions though: she wanted to know where this Frankie hung out. She'd find him, with all the other junkies, around the city boardwalk to the east of the bridge, Rebecca had told her. Look hard enough, that's where he'll be.

⚊

Bailey entered the coffee shop of the art museum, housed in all its modernity in a military hospital that dated back to the seventeenth century. He didn't go for arty stuff that much, although he had been here once before with an old girlfriend: Tanya, free-spirited, veggie, arty, yoga-loving and stunningly gorgeous. She'd been perfect. But Bailey couldn't do perfect. That was pressure; that was boring. As he ordered coffee, designer sandwiches and an assortment of cakes – anything he thought Frankie might eat – he spotted him, sitting at a table in the corner, looking out of place in his tracksuit and scruffy trainers, a hovering security guard keeping him in his sights.

Bailey approached and placed the tray of food on the table. "You don't look too good, Frankie," he said, sitting down. "Did you get fixed up at the Riverside?"

Frankie was not in the mood for niceties. The pains in his arms and legs were worse than ever, and even in the heat of the gallery café he couldn't get warm.

"Don't go acting all concerned, ya fake bollix! I'm going in for the maintenance when I can. That's all I can risk right now."

"You can't keep hiding, Frankie – or sleeping rough." Bailey could see the kid was exhausted. "I can try and fix you up with somewhere."

"I have a place to kip. It'll do for now," Frankie snapped. "I take it the grub is for sharing?"

"Help yourself," Bailey said, sliding the tray towards him. He glanced round at his surroundings – clean blonde and chrome furniture, abstract art on the walls. "I like your choice of venue. You into art, Mr Harte?"

Frankie put a whole doughnut into his mouth and spoke while still chewing. "I'm into breathing. That is all." He continued shovelling the food into his mouth.

Bailey watched in silence, pushing his own uneaten sandwiches towards Frankie and waiting patiently.

"There's an exhibition on here," Frankie said eventually. "It's called HEARTH – millions of photographs of buildings all clustered together." He seemed to chew with some discomfort, Bailey noticed. "Paper city, savage looking!"

"So what's it all about?" Bailey prompted quietly, his eyes drawn to the scabby stumps on Frankie's hand.

"Ever heard of metaphor?" Frankie asked, still snapping.

Bailey didn't take the bait. He was in no mood to play at philosophy with a junkie, no matter how fascinating it might be. He tried again. "My offer still stands. I can get you protection."

Frankie stopped eating and grimaced, his complexion turning a strange shade of violet. He looked distinctly uncomfortable, trying, and failing miserably, to stifle a series of gut-wrenching belches.

"Like I said before, thanks but no thanks."

"Your choice, son – but you have to know the danger you are in." Bailey could feel the heat of his irritation rising, and it bothered him. In this business, emotions were only reserved for the personal space, even the negative ones. "Frankie, was Collins involved with The Poet? Did he do business for that prick?"

Frankie shook his head, though it was a *not listening* shake as opposed to a *don't know* shake.

"There were strange marks on his body – we can't quite figure out what they are."

Bailey pulled a photograph out of the inside pocket of his jacket and placed it in front of Frankie. It showed the dead boy's back, a series of puncture wounds on his buttery dead flesh, running like train tracks down each side of his spine. Frankie glanced at the photo, and Bailey noticed how he shuddered at the sight of it.

"Banana bricks," Frankie quipped, averting his eyes. "The Poet owns a couple of warehouses just off the M50 though you'll never trace it to him. There's a builder's providers in one of them. Every now and then he has a special delivery – one coming up this Friday. Gear will be in the cavity blocks that he has delivered from Asia or fuck knows where."

Bailey failed miserably at masking his surprise. "And you know this how?"

"I hear things, as *you* well know, or you wouldn't be here buying me hipster snacks. This body might be wrecked but my mind's not completely fucked – not yet anyway." Frankie lifted the remaining cake and sandwiches, wrapped them in paper napkins and stuffed them into his pockets. "And I always was a good listener." He stood up, rubbing his legs back to life before clumsily zipping up his tracksuit top and pulling the hood up. "Don't follow me out yet. Some interesting stuff in here, so take your time, Dicktective – enjoy some culture."

Unsteady on his feet, he headed for the exit, turning heads on high alert as he concealed his face beneath the hood. Bailey couldn't stop the smile that formed as he watched Frankie gain distance from the grandeur of his surroundings with that familiar Ratso Rizzo swagger.

The smile didn't last long. By the look of him, Frankie was on borrowed time and there was nothing Bailey could do about it.

⅄

She had always thanked the universe for the absence of photographs from her youth and that she came from an age before social media, with its selfies and slut-shaming sneakies that could be created instantly, yet tormented you forever. Back then she had probably scared people, the way she looked. It had been pretty bad, to be in that skin, and behind her eyes, even with her new life, that wasted image haunted her. How could she ever forget? The mirror never lies, no matter how you think you are facing the world. The inner world of your soul, the part of you that nobody else knows, is always there, ready to remind you of what you really are.

She squeezes shut her dry, sore eyes now and clenches her teeth against the ache of her damaged spirit and the festering sore gouged to the bone, always with her, with no other purpose than to remind her of what she had come from.

I dream.

Of Jesse's father, his face as vivid as if he was right there with me, once more, the man who took me under his wing when he found me in my rock bottom place.

Street kids seek no company, except for other street kids. It's safer to hang out with the devil you know than to be alone. The hostels are dangerous places for young girls – or indeed young boys. The tough and the dominant rule the roost and take from the weakest anything they want. Nothing is sacred; nothing is off limits.

Once the victim, the lesson never needs to be learned twice.

⁂

Since talking to that Rebecca girl, Beth had been coming into town every day, and most nights, hanging out at the boardwalk along the city quays. Luke's calls went unanswered, voicemails ignored, texts unread; his 'Call me' notes lay scattered on the hall floor where they had landed through her letterbox. Was that cruel of her? Beth didn't have the strength, not the peace of mind, to call it. She was preoccupied – with the girl Rebecca and what to make of her.

She was certainly pretty, alluring and mature for her age, but there was something else behind her eyes – tension of some kind. She was no doubt shaken by Jesse's death, but she was also cold – a cold creature. Perhaps, as she had hinted, her parents were violent. That might explain it. Sizing her up though – the cut of her, her confidence, the nice, affluent house she lived in – it just didn't add up.

Fear was palpable, as was stress and anxiety. But not from this one. There was something in the girl that Beth recognised – a steel reserve, a disconnect that made Beth wonder, over and over, what her lovely boy had been so attracted to, what she had that he had needed so much, besides the sex. Could that have been all?

At least Rebecca had given her something to go on, so Beth would leave her alone for now. She had somewhere else to go looking first, somewhere else to direct her attention.

⟁

She can't for the life of her feel anything. It's like her organs are made of rubber and her skin is sprayed with Teflon. She's pinched herself in all the right places, the sensitive bits, the soft white flesh under her arms, inside her thighs, on her breasts; nothing, not even a flinch, despite the mottled purplish mess that her own cruel fingers have left on her skin. She even boiled the kettle and poured it over her hand. The water steamed off her flesh, sizzled, and yes, there was a certain satisfactory throb and burn that she relished, a reprieve from the pressure that was building underneath, unrelenting, as was the white noise, so loud at night. And when the blisters had risen, oh that wonderful sensation of bursting them, pricking the translucent skin with a knife, the pent-up moisture spitting out, erupting with a delicious rush. And she pulled it back, the skin, a layer of her agony, her vexation, her frustration revealed, red raw beneath the flesh, as I am.

⟁

Drunk and dishevelled, a crusty old man was causing hassle. Beth watched him, his skin as flabby as his clothes, shouting nonsense and stumbling into the personal space of everyone in his path - until he was pushed down into a seat by an irritated police officer threatening him with a cell if he didn't shut up and stay still. The gruffness of the law went right over her head as she took in everything she could see around her: a young guy with a filthy backpack still strapped to him, sprawled comatose on the bench opposite her, while another one sat close by, huddled on the floor, moaning. She tried not to stare as she stood at the incident desk, anxiously waiting to be noticed by the uniformed officer behind it. When he failed to pay her any attention, she spoke up.

"I'm here in relation to my son's death," she told him. "My son – Jesse Downes – overdose – last Friday week." The words cut from her throat, jagged broken glass.

The desk officer looked at her now, bags prematurely established under his youthful eyes as he typed the details she gave him on the desktop keyboard. He seemed like a nice man, so Beth took the chance to ask about this young fella, Frankie, and how she had been given his name by a friend of Jesse's.

"All I know is that he – he hangs out around the boardwalk."

"And hundreds like him," the officer replied, gesturing over her head at another policeman while pointing at the disruptive old man – *Move him out of here* – before focusing on Beth once more. "Look, you really shouldn't be doing that, asking around and all. It's very dangerous out there for someone like you. I'm sorry Mrs Downes, but all I can do is forward on the information for your son's file."

Beth could feel every nerve in her body begin to vibrate.

"My son is dead. Please – no one is telling me anything."

No longer able to trust her legs to support her weight, Beth clutched the edge of the desk, her fingertips pressed white against the countertop.

The officer frowned. "Hang on a sec," he muttered and typed hurriedly. "Bailey, Detective Bailey would be the man in charge. I'll leave a note for him to contact you."

He was already looking over her shoulder again and she followed his gaze, gawking blatantly as two policemen guided a spaced-out teenager towards the desk; blood oozed from the kid's head. The desk telephone rang sharply, jolting Beth back from the sight.

"They'll be doing all they can," the officer assured her before answering the phone. "I'm sorry for your loss, really. If anything comes of it, they'll be in touch."

If anything comes of it? Beth watched him make notes about his new and more important conversation. She had been dismissed.

She turned to leave, finding herself once again staring at the drugged-up teenager, now bent over, head down as he struggled not to slide off the chair and she found herself wondering about his mother, about her story. The desk officer's voice, harsher now, cut into her thoughts. "Mrs Downes, please, you'll have to move away now!"

She left the station, still wondering about that other boy, that other mother, and wondering if her fate was to be as catastrophic as Beth's own.

ᛉ

Sixteen. She had once been an eager student of survival, hanging out in parts of the city that ordinary people don't see – the underbelly, the bowels of dereliction where she stashed her blankets during the day while she kept moving, scurrying, learning quickly how to avoid the police, the social services, the cookie monsters, the plain crazy people.

She did the odd hand job – for a fix, a meal, a favour – a get-out-of-jail wank. Eating and staying warm and dry were her only priorities, until *he* came and everything changed. Panic had altered her perception, changed her as she puked day and night, haunted by her unborn child. And now she will be haunted forever by her lovely dead boy.

I wait for her, and *I* feel it, all of it.

The slow and heavy weight she carries as she sees him in the shadows, in the corner of her eye, in the grey of night and the blink between dusk and dawn, and she moves slowly, plodding, an amputee. Crooked and unbalanced from the part of her that is missing.

ᛉ

The box body truck had only begun to reverse out through the gates at the rear of the building provisions warehouse when screaming sirens and screeching cars zoomed in to block the vehicle's path. Police officers in practised formations secured the front and rear of the industrial unit while Bailey and Rourke emerged from an unmarked car and followed their uniformed counterparts in through the rear.

Inside, two men, already in handcuffs, hurled abusive threats in heavy eastern European accents without a shred of fear. Rourke told them to *Shut-the-fuck-up* while Bailey surveyed opened pallets of funereal headstones and cavity bricks and freshly packed crates of bananas, one already dismantled by his colleagues to reveal the drugs hidden inside them.

Scrutinising the contents of a small office, he noted weighing scales and half-filled sacks of brick dust and sugar. Neat cylinders of heroin were stacked in high piles ready to go, along with boxes filled with pellets of white powder and pocket-sized clear plastic bags of coloured pills in pretty pastel shades – deadly shades.

"Frankie boy made good this time!" Rourke blurted out, a little too loudly for Bailey's liking as the two men in handcuffs were shoved past them towards the exit. The men turned to scowl at Rourke.

Once they were out of sight Bailey grabbed Rourke by his lapels, pent-up rage suddenly taking over him. "Why don't you take your own advice and shut-the-fuck-up! And say your prayers that you haven't put that mother-fucking grim reaper on the kid's back!"

⚔

A few blocks away, the sirens still wailing trouble in the distance, Darren gathered his muddy football gear, waved goodbye to some straggling team mates and walked out through the school gates, his bulging schoolbag hanging off his shoulder. He barely had time to note the colour of the van that crept up alongside him, its side door sliding open as a guzz-eyed, squat little man jumped into his path and smiled at him.

Darren knew immediately what this was about. You can't mess with people like Rebecca.

He tried to make a run for it. A pointless gesture, he knew, but the fear of what might happen inside that van propelled him to make the attempt. Guzz-eye was ready, way ahead of Darren, dancing with him on the footpath while a second guy, pure rage and dirty-inked forearms, emerged from the van. In a matter of seconds, all that was left on the street was Darren's schoolbag and the smell of burning rubber.

⚓

It began. The warm frisson from coming down, the burn surging through her veins, a cocktail of adrenalin, of exhilaration; of pain. Seeking out those parts of her, the secret parts that hid so well, hunkered there in the labyrinth of her core. The secret parts that wait, muffled in their whispered longings, bound and gagged, cold and remote in the restless anticipation of this glorious moment. The moment of submissive acceptance, of this strange, spiking warmth that oozed, flowed and throbbed to tranquilize the ache that itched, now unhooked, the itch of fire and longing, of wrought and wrath, crashing through those last, most stubborn fragments of resistance. Cutting deep to the marrow, digging, digging as the relentless dither of the hollow came unleashed. Without the burn, she would implode, she would be lost. She would be nothing.

Rebecca's piercings were oozing a little bit. She felt no pain though, the adrenaline rush numbing it so that all she experienced was pure, brutal pleasure. She had reached the plateau, that sense of invincibility, as she hung there, resurrection-style, her weight evenly balanced by the chain-linked hooks that her fellow marionettes had carefully pierced through her flesh. Once more, the metal hooks had opened wounds that had healed over so many times, raised white scars, three in a row and equal distance apart, running down each side of her belly from her breasts. Rebecca was pumped; she had been anticipating this suspension for weeks now. She had planned to bring Jesse along, but damn, was she glad now that she hadn't. What had she been thinking! He wouldn't have been able to handle it. Poor bastard.

The club, fronted by a humble little book shop in the centre of town, was hers, all hers. Secretly known to crew members as Fantocinnis, a code word that Rebecca was proud to have thought up herself, the place held no more than fifty people seated. The shell of a disused theatre that she rented from an ancient actor friend she'd met at some charity event, a boring wine reception that her mother had begged her to accompany her to; she couldn't be trusted to stay sober on her own, and Pops was eager for her to represent him with a nice juicy donation. Rebecca had been drawn to the garish outfit and pervy nature of the owner, whom she nicknamed Relic, and he had been drawn to her too. Much like the Relic, the theatre was a remnant from the seventies when independent groups of performers had rebelled against the format of established traditional plays by staging productions in the back rooms of pubs and restaurants, even public parks, and challenging audiences with their new approaches. The stage at Fantocinnis was tiny, but it didn't matter. The important fixtures were the beams high above that had originally supported the make-and-do lighting rigs. They were perfect for Rebecca and her suspension junkies: solid, sound, safely supporting them as under watchful eyes, Rebecca's gang of marionettes ensured that each other's hook-ups went off without any problems.

To add spice to the experience, they often had an audience, who watched from the old plush seats in the auditorium. Some liked very much to watch, non-participating voyeurs, like her Relic. Rebecca tolerated him, and he waived the rent. There were others, a general menagerie of misfits, and that was okay too, once they had been screened and warned, and showed they were willing to pay for the privilege.

'Rising from death' was the theme of her current position, her body curving backwards, facing the ceiling, letting her head fall back and totally abandoning herself to the pose. Holding her breath for as long as possible, tense against the pulling force on the skin and muscle of her stomach. And there she hung, swaying gently, a doll-like puppet, principal marionette, deliciously light-headed and enjoying the prolonged, orgasmic rush.

The thud and thump of heavy metal music pounded in her ears, drowning out the rattle of the chains that hung from the rafters, suspending her, pulling against the weight of her own body. The pain would come later – after the hooks were removed, but even then the adrenaline would anaesthetise it for a while.

And she needed to release this pent-up energy – this bad fucking energy. Too much stress these days, and stupid little bastards who should know better. And now that silly fucker Darren, telling on her like that. Just as well she had scheduled a slot here in her underground club. Her tribe at Fantocinnis cared about each other but knew to keep their mouths shut. That was why they came here and why it remained a secret and so protected, known only to a select crew. Trust was the most important factor for the members of the club, especially when life, or death, was at stake.

If you broke the trust, you suffered.

It was Rebecca's number one rule, and she made an example of anyone who breached it.

As her chains were released and she was deposited safely onto a mattress on the stage with a heavy blanket placed over her, her mind was momentarily stripped of every other thing as she came down from the biggest adrenalin rush she had ever had. It really did get better, the riskier the hook, and she felt powerful too, braver than ever before. Shaking out her limbs, she could already feel her nerves begin to tingle with the pain that would surely rise as she came down, but that was okay too. Pain is not always a bad thing.

As she sat up, drowsy with pleasure and enjoying the afterglow of the rush, she used a makeshift first-aid kit of antiseptic wipes and sticking plasters to gently clean and cover her freshly pierced wounds, humming a soothing tune to herself.

Just blocks away, a van screeched to a halt and Darren, the cause of her recent sleepless nights, was shoved out onto the road back where he started, outside the school gates. The vehicle sped off into the night, leaving the boy beaten raw, bleeding on the tarmac, his nose smashed and pushed into his swollen face. Darren dragged himself up to sit on the kerb, sniffling back snot, blood and tears, the words of the thug still echoing inside his throbbing skull: *A favour for a friend.*

Rebecca sniffed indignantly as her phone beeped a text message: *Job done.*

No indeed, pain was not always a bad thing.

⋏

So let's talk about Jesse's father. I can still remember the first time I saw him. Nearly twenty years my senior, he was good looking in that lazy kind of way that creeps up on you, so slowly that you only notice how green his eyes are when they peer into your soul until you can hardly breathe. And those long black eyelashes, sweeping down as he moves in to kiss you for the first time; soft lips and practised tongue, smelling good and always immaculate in his sharp expensive suits and good shoes. Perfection in the detail. If you didn't know him, you'd never guess he came from those shit-bag flats, heroin city, his expensive aftershave wafting around him like an inviting sea breeze that momentarily helped me to forget the piss-pot stink that emanated from my clothes, my hair; my skin.

He was different alright. Clever, but I didn't cop on to that until it was too late, until I was in too deep – and too out of it – to realise the kind of game he played and what he was doing to me.

What he saw in me back then I'll never understand – or maybe I can. It was her he saw; the way she knew ... but that was eighteen years ago. Then, she had been just fifteen years old, a skinny little girl-child; a runner. Running from dysfunction and finding nothing but.

⚓

No white, no red; nothing that might suggest a funereal vibe. Luke had chosen Citrus Sunrise, a neatly packaged spray of coral, orange and yellow roses as he took a leap of faith today in making his umpteenth attempt to visit Beth. Relieved when she finally let him in, he sidled past her, the bunch of flowers wedged into the crook of his elbow and carrying groceries, the handles of the plastic bags biting into his fingers.

"Rescue these, please, before I squash whatever life is left of them!" he said.

Reluctantly she took the already wilting roses to go in search of some kind of vessel to stuff them into. He squirmed, biting his tongue, aware that every word was a potential trigger. How he worried about upsetting her, offending her; eggshells.

He had noticed the bandage, carelessly wrapped around the four fingers of her left hand.

"What happened there?" he asked, not sure at all if he had managed to mask his reaction to the odorous mess in the kitchen, or the state of her, his usually fastidious assistant. Beth didn't seem at all phased by the filth or the fact that he was a witness to it. Stale uneaten food lay on the counter-tops. The sink was blocked by something unidentified, the waste bin spilling over, and every dish she owned had been used and left where it lay, some of it ending up smashed on the floor amid sticky floor spills. On her dining table were mouldy coffee mugs, their stains leaving rings on batches of unopened bills. No welcome in this house, once cherished; no longer.

He took off his coat and got to work, cleaning as best he could, disinfecting the drain and filling the kitchen sink with soapy liquid. His hopes rose when she pulled from some-where beneath the mess a clean dish towel and began to dry off the items that he washed. Dip, wipe, rinse and dry, the repetition strangely comforting and neither of them spoke again until some semblance of order had returned to her small living space and, he hoped, to her troubled, grief-worn mind.

"Now, a marathon cleaning session deserves strong coffee with some chocolate éclairs," he said cheerfully. "There's a box of them somewhere in one of these shopping bags. If you make the coffee, I'll fish for the goodies!"

The cakes, when he found them, were rather battered, but Beth made an effort to smile in appreciation of his thoughtfulness. Foolishly, that flicker of light on her face was enough to prompt him do what he swore to himself he wouldn't do – embrace her. But as he made his involuntary attempt, she adeptly dodged him by fetching two clean mugs from the cupboard and busying herself unpacking groceries.

"You're probably here about the job," she said suddenly keeping her back to him. "I do understand – you have to replace me, so don't feel that you—"

He gently put his hand on her arm. "Your job will be waiting. Take however long you need. I have a temp covering for you, so don't worry – your meticulous filing has not gone to ruin."

He whisked instant coffee with milk and poured it first into her mug and then his own, before adding the hot water and two heaped spoons of sugar to his coffee.

"You've been very good, Mr Thompson. Thank you. I don't deserve it." She seemed to choke on the words.

Still she would not call him by his first name. He blinked slowly. "I'm here for you, Beth. You have to know that by now?"

The question hung in the air as Luke stood awkwardly, averting his eyes from her while inside he cringed. *Idiot!* Once again he was wearing his heart on his sleeve.

She left the kitchen, saving him from any further blundering declarations, however heartfelt. Distracted, he followed her into the sitting room – the front parlour she called it – and his gaze settled on the wall of photographs. A sea of faces – young Jesse in school uniform; Jesse as a toddler on Beth's lap on a visit to Santa; a young Beth in a photo booth holding baby Jesse; Jesse at the zoo; Jesse in the park. A pictorial shrine to Jesse.

Yet all Luke could see was the boy's cold, hard stare.

"So, since you mentioned it, have you given any thought to coming back to work, just a couple of hours a day even?" he asked gently.

Beth took his coffee mug from him and marched back out into the kitchen. She tipped his coffee down the drain, a clear sign for him to go. "I need more time."

"Of course, though it would be good for you to get back to—"

Beth suddenly slammed the mugs into the sink, shattering one against the stainless steel.

"I checked in at the police station," she said, her shoulders rising, sharp, full of tension. "They're fucking useless! The scum who gave my boy that poison is out there and they're not doing a damn thing about it."

This time, as he moved to comfort her, Beth let him and sank into his arms. And he saw that she had bitten her lip as a trickle of blood seeped out into the fabric of his crisp, white shirt.

⋏

He had taken her, like so many other runaways, under his wing. He gave her shelter, food, clothes, and he kept the curs away, the scumbag predators who spent their nights searching for the likes of her. Pubescent, desperate wretches, running from abuse, but too stupid to see that it was omnipresent, lurking behind every corner, every dead-end laneway; every good turn demanding payback. And he had been no different. There was always a debt to be paid, so she dealt for him, ran errands for him, provided other... services. But by the

74

time she realised the debt was never-ending, she was well and truly sucked in to his world.

They were only connected for a short while – maybe six months – but from the outset, he had represented something else for her, the father-figure, the protector, the gladiator fighting her battles, the lover she had childishly fantasised about. But oh man, would she learn.

He spoke softly and with an intelligence that beguiled her. He read books, books she longed to own for herself but couldn't afford. She more than made up for that later.

He told her that she was pretty, sexy, bought her nice clothes and perfume and make-up and took her to nightclubs where the doormen never questioned her age. Sometimes, when she caught a glimpse of herself in a mirror she was able to forget that she was a useless, unloved piece of shit.

And he could be tender, almost caring. He needed her to trust him, after all. But she never really got to know him, never got under the surface of that polished veneer. That was something he never allowed.

⅄

Shrouded in grey, Beth stepped off the bus. Her complexion was ashen, that washed-out lack-of-sleep colour, and her eyes were sunk in blue-black sockets – the shadow-self. She was wearing Jesse's jeans, the ends turned up hobo-like over her boots, the waist cinched tightly with a belt. The silver-grey coat rendered her ghost-like, almost invisible as she walked slowly along the quay wall, lost and despondent, indifferent about her own safety. She stopped to watch a group of youths, all pale faces, sharp limbs and rotten teeth. Some quenched their thirst with cans of beer, the cheap-as-shite variety, others lost in their own private dance, swayed on their feet; stoned from their horrible realities.

The kids who accompanied them ran wild, the shriek of their playfulness searing like bile in her gullet. She watched as a police car cruised into the picture and two uniformed officers, one male, one female, emerged to disperse the group. She couldn't take her eyes away as one of the junkie boys, completely wasted, began to hurl abuse at them – *Are ya ridin' that fuckin' Banner?* When they moved in to question him, he continued with his tirade, shoving and posturing until they backed him against the wall and searched him. That shut him up. Didn't he know how futile all that false bravado was?

Beth kept watching, mesmerised, as a young woman with an infant in a pushchair entered the scene, yelling at the officers when they pointed towards the baby girl. But she became hysterical when the female officer reached in to grapple with the child's clothing, pulling at her disposable nappy, the baby screeching in discomfort as several small plastic packets were retrieved from inside it. Beth couldn't take in what she had just seen, how undaunted everyone was as the drama continued to unfold – the couple arrested and pushed into the police car with the crying baby, its scrawny bare legs still exposed; the door closed and the car sped away.

Staring after them, Beth gasped in small fitful breaths, still trying to process what she had just witnessed. She propped herself against the wall as the river flowed past her, cold and fast, out towards the bay. As she closed her eyes to the lure of it, she turned once more to focus on the group of youths, oblivious to what had just happened, most of them brazenly strung out. Talking at once, an incoherent jabber laced with the nasal whine of damaged membranes, they squabbled over cigarettes and other items they could sell or barter, occasionally tapping passers-by for loose change; *Giz yer odds, Mister! I need four euro for the hostel. I have to pay for me prescription, here, look at it. I swear it's for me meds!*

And as she stood there, entranced by the shenanigans, she hardly noticed the first push. The second shove, however, a little more forceful, made her whirl round on her heels. There stood a girl – late teens perhaps, though it was hard to tell from her emaciated body – squaring up to Beth, blocking her path.

"What are you looking at?" the girl snarled, hostile and nervous all in one.

Beth took her time to respond, assessing the danger, taking in her inquisitor's appearance. She was nothing but a pale string-bean, apart from her protruding stomach, the dark circles under her eyes mirroring Beth's own. Her eyes were glassy, pupils dilated, and she reeked of dirty sweat. Beth involuntarily moved her head back, turning her nose up as the girl moved closer, and she felt bad for doing that as the girl so obviously noticed.

"I've seen you before. The only ones who keep hanging around here are looking for something – so what the fuck do you want?" The girl paused to look around her, unsteady on her feet. "Maybe I can help you?" she added quietly, her words slurred.

Beth saw her chance. "Or maybe I can help you?" she said quickly.

The girl tensed up. "Are you one of those religious nut jobs or something – come here to save me from meself?"

She watched Beth put her hand in her pocket and take out a twenty euro note.

"Do you know a fella called Frankie, he hangs out here?" Beth asked, offering her the money.

The girl wasted no time. She snatched the note and pushed Beth against the low quay wall, slapping her hard across her face. "If you scream, I'll fuck you in the bleedin' river, right!" She kneed Beth hard in the groin and jabbed a spindly elbow into her stomach, wedging it there while she rifled Beth's pockets, taking her mobile phone and the remainder of her cash. As she loosened her grip to stash the spoils down her pants, Beth regained her composure and grabbed her attacker's thin ponytail. Shrieking loudly, the girl tried to free herself, her nails digging into the back of Beth's hand. They fell to the ground, grappling with each other until Beth overpowered her and pinned her arms down.

"Some help here! Please!" Beth screamed out, but people just kept on walking, avoiding eye contact, paying no attention to the ridiculous scene or to the plight of the young girl. Even the other junkies had deftly moved out of sight.

Beth reclaimed her phone and money and, standing up, was about to call the police when the girl began to wail: "Fuckin' cunt – you hurt me baby!"

The words pierced Beth to the core. She stopped long enough to take a good look at the girl, still slumped on the ground, moaning and writhing. "Go on, get the bleedin' cops? I might get a fuckin' dry bed for the night."

Beth lowered the phone, the girl's predicament sinking in, and held out her hand to help her to her feet. "What about the hostels?" was all she could think of to ask as the girl clutched her belly and winced.

"How do you think this fuckin' happened?" she yelled angrily, attempting to walk away. "Those fuckin' kips aren't safe for the likes of me. I'll take me bleedin' chances on the streets."

She had barely finished the sentence when she doubled over and collapsed. Beth watched a dark stain appear between the girl's legs, seeping through her light-coloured jeans. Horrified, she tried to flag down a taxi. When one finally stopped, and the driver refused to get out and help the girl, Beth hauled her up off the ground herself, wrapped her in the grey coat, pushed her into the taxi and without hesitation got in beside her.

⚔

The city was different back then – greyer, colder, poorer. The streets weren't filled with the wealth and cosmopolitan energy that came later. Nowadays, there is a feeling that there is no money, but *I* don't buy that. It isn't everywhere, it never was. The people who have it are hoarding. Scared to spend, that's all. He had it in buckets, though he was never scared. Not of anyone. She had been sick for some time, and he, knowing fuck all about women, put her persistent illness down to the drugs. He regularly got her stoned, you see, so she would do stuff to him, kinky stuff that made her feel like she was dead and made him feel alive inside; killing love. She had learned to believe him when he told her how to feel, and how to be, so she wasn't even that concerned when her period didn't come that first month, or the second. She was pretty strung out most of the time, and her body didn't always function the way it ought to. When there was no show on the third month, though, and she cupped her tiny, swollen belly, she knew. She never let on, not to anyone, just went about her daily business, his business, hanging around the usual haunts while she tried to force her brain in gear just enough to make the right decision.

A

The smell of nurturing overwhelmed her as she moved through the maternity ward. Beth's gaze lingered far too long on a breastfeeding mother with her pink, wrinkled new-born cradled in her arms. That scent – of birth, of babies, of lactating mothers – brought tears to her eyes, and took her right back to that moment, when she had been reborn.

Beth gave a cry of laboured yearning – she couldn't help herself – and the mother glared back at her with suspicion.

Hold it together.

She walked on, her gaze skimming over another new mammy perched on the edge of her bed, peering in wonder at the sleeping miracle in the cot beside her. The woman turned and smiled at her, the smile fading quickly when she saw the expression on Beth's face, and she leaned across her sleeping child as if to shield it.

Beth wanted to reassure the woman that she meant no harm, that she would keep her longing, her envy, in check. But how could she trust herself now?

Soft-footed, she approached the bed tucked into the furthest corner. Beth found the street junkie there, behind a sky-blue, pleated polyester curtain and sat down on a plastic chair beside her. She wondered why they put the poor girl in here. Surely it was an added torment on top of what she had just been through.

She read the name on the chart at the end of the bed: Nellie X, now moaning and sniffling in her half-sleep. Beth took her hand and uttered nonsensical words, the kind of sounds reserved for soothing a sick child. It was all she could think of to do as she sat there and the hours passed and the ward turned quieter, darker, babies and mothers drifting off to sleep in the heat of the safe space. And Nellie whimpered on while Beth listened until, finally, the girl opened her eyes.

"I'm sorry. I'm so sorry," Beth whispered urgently.

She was taken completely by surprise when Nellie sat up, reached for a beaker of water and swallowed it down in one go before clearing her throat with a raspy cough. "Don't be," she said. "You did me a favour. I didn't have the bottle to fix it."

No explanation was needed; there was an understanding in the tight clasping of each other's hand, the connection only broken when Beth pulled away to rummage in her pockets. She placed all the money she was carrying onto the bedside locker as silently, she urged Nellie to get clean. Though she knew better than to say such a thing out loud.

"I hope you'll be okay," she whispered and got up to leave.

Nellie grabbed her sleeve. "Are you really Frankie's family?" she asked, barely able to keep her eyes open.

"Yes," Beth lied, chewing once again on the torn flesh inside her mouth.

Nellie pulled her closer, one final moment of connection. "Leave me your phone number. Frankie'll get the word that you're looking for him."

She understood that line, that in-between place of invisible poverty. Her mother had had nothing, although at least she had always had a roof over her head. But sometimes that roof keeps a lid on the worst kind of home, and true poverty can have nothing to do with lack of money.

When matted knots of dirty hair go untangled; when toes bleed because shoes are too small; when knickers washed at night are pulled on, still damp, in the morning because they are the only pair she has, a little girl starts to understand neglect. When she makes her way to school exhausted because there's been a strange man in the house, or because a drunken fight has gone on all night; when teachers think she's just plain lazy because she falls asleep in class; when she relies on the generosity of classmates to share their lunch with her or go hungry – these are the things that let a child know she's different.

So when, from somewhere deep inside, she heard a tiny voice calling out for help despite her shattered sense of self-worth, she knew it was time to run.

⚓

Frankie swept his eyes in all directions, scanning for trouble as he neared the boardwalk. Nellie's story sounded like a crock of shit – a woman from his family looking for him? There could only be one woman, and Frankie hadn't seen her since his father had been shot, when she had run off and left him on his own – well, not exactly on his own; with his grandmother. For fuck's sake, like he was going to stick around and wreck an old lady's life too.

Still, his heart lifted at the idea that his mother might be looking for him. Maybe she wanted to come back, maybe she wanted them to be together again. Family, yeah? Or maybe she was dying, or had come into some money and wanted to share it with him – to get him off the streets, get him clean.

Not fucking likely.

He trusted Nellie though, so it was worth the risk to see what this was all about. Still keeping sketch for familiar faces, or unwelcome ones, he awkwardly lit a cigarette with his left hand. This southpaw shit was going to take some getting used to; at least he was remembering that his fingers were no longer there – phantom fingers to reach out for his phantom mother.

He could see someone like her coming towards him now, though she was covered up in an auld one's scarf and a shapeless raincoat. It couldn't be his mother; she wouldn't be caught dead looking like this bag lady. Always the glamour girl, his ma; even the monthly children's allowance was blown on hairdos, new shoes and fucking handbags. Still, he couldn't quell the hope that it might be her, that she suddenly felt some sense of loyalty to him, or just plain missed her only child, and was back to make amends, back to make family.

Frankie stood up straight as she approached, his heart racing as she came straight towards him, rudely staring at his mutilated hand. With her face shrouded in darkness, she called his name, but her voice was too low for him to be sure. Against his better judgement he moved towards her, edgy with a mix of anticipation and dread.

"Frankie? Is your name Frankie?" she asked again.

"Who the fuck *are* you?" he yelled, disappointment and suspicion washing over him. "Fuck off. I'm not dealing – and you can tell Nellie I'll get her for this!"

"I'm not buying," the woman replied, her tone cooler this time. "And don't blame Nellie – I tricked her."

Frankie dragged on his cigarette, taking a moment to size her up, to suss out the danger. One thing he knew for sure from the cut of her: she wasn't brass.

"What do you want, Lady?"

"It's kind of personal. Someone gave me your name."

"Nellie? Yeah, you said. Why? Why did she put you on to me?"

"No. Not her. Look, I just need to ask you some questions."

He shook his head. "I don't answer questions. Now get going. Don't you know this place is rife with junkies and thieves?"

She didn't respond, didn't move. He could feel the tension oozing out of her. "Please? Just a couple of minutes of your time. I'll pay you," she said.

Frankie laughed. "Jesus, Lady – sorry, a shag's out of the question!"

She squirmed, her eyes almost popping with consternation, until he smiled and she seemed to relax a little.

"Look, Lady, tell you what – just for Nellie, because she's a good skin," Frankie gestured towards a fast-food outlet across the street. "Over there, a burger and a coffee will buy you ten minutes. You can tell me what this is all about and I'll get fed, and there'll be witnesses if you turn out to be a psycho bitch."

He darted across the road before she could agree, and went inside the brightly lit restaurant. He found a seat close to the window and watched her as she hesitated, shuffling with uncertainty, before crossing the road to follow him in.

⅄

Beth watched, fascinated, while Frankie chewed huge chunks of burger and bap, the entire thing disappearing in moments.

"Aren't you going to eat that?" he asked, pointing at her tray.

She pushed it towards him. "I have that effect on people," he quipped, reaching for her chips and veggie wrap. "Don't mind if I do."

"What happened to you?" she asked, staring at the stumps of his missing fingers.

Frankie ignored her question. "Let me guess," he said, "you're a writer, itching for authenticity for your novel. Or you're a reporter ... or one of those fake do-gooders on the telly looking to do an in-depth documentary on street kids in Ireland. First Nellie, now me. Show the world how human we are, how pitiful, then fuck off with your film in the can and your eye on the awards? Yeah, am I close?"

Beth struggled for a suitable response. He was a smart kid, with the same soft edges of burgeoning manhood as Jesse. Though Frankie's features were serrated by sleeping rough and abusing drugs, she could see that under the unhealthy pallor, he was quite a looker. He acted like a hard man, but his blue eyes gave him away; vulnerable and scared. As she studied him closely, the madness of the situation almost made her forget why she was there in the first place, and she found herself wondering who this young guy was, where he came from – how he ended up this way, so much so that she didn't even hear the last sentence he had uttered, his mouth still full of food as Frankie got back on his feet, ready to leave.

Panicking, she grabbed his sleeve. "How old are you?"

He jerked his arm loose. "Lady, only a detective can ask me that!"

"My boy was seventeen. Look! I have a photo!"

As she fumbled in her pocket to retrieve her picture of Jesse, Frankie moved closer to the door. She blocked him, thrusting the photo into his face.

He wouldn't look at it, but kept his eyes on her, perplexed. "Go home, Lady, you're not in your right mind."

Hands in pockets, he nudged her out of the way with his shoulder and quickly moved out into the street. She followed, struggling to keep up as he strode away, her frustration mounting when he refused to stop and listen.

"Jesse died – from an overdose!" she yelled.

Passing strangers glanced at her before moving on.

"The drugs," she screamed after him, "he got them from you!"

Frankie stopped and suddenly turned back, Beth almost colliding with him. Gasping for breath, she held out the photograph again and this time he took it from her. He studied it beneath the street light, his brow creased with apprehension. Then he pushed her roughly into the dark recess of a shop doorway. She cowered, her arms up in defence.

"You'd better fuck off now, for your own sake – you hear me?" he said, leaning in close to her face.

He stepped back, his teeth clenched in a threatening sneer, and she squeezed her eyes shut, prepared for a blow, or the slash of a knife – but it didn't come, and when she opened her eyes again, he was gone, vanished out into the crowd as she lowered her arms, shaken but unhurt to retrieve Jesse's photo from the dirty, wet footpath.

By the time she had fallen into his lair he was more than twice her age, his fortune slowly and steadily amassing from laundering money he'd invested in the city's club circuit. The economic boom was in its infancy and he, the consummate business man, was there from the get-go, scooping up derelict buildings on the cheap and biding his time until the right investment opportunity came along. Vultures have always lived here.

With his money and his encroaching power, and in all his camouflaged finery, he had dragged himself from the gutter and made something of himself, but that didn't seem to make him any more compassionate to others at the bottom of the heap. For on his way up, he carried deep within him a twisted moment, a moment that changed him, colouring every cruelty he instigated. And I doubt if he ever gave a second thought to the pathetic kids who wore out the pavements day and night, selling his merchandise and dutifully handing over the profits.

Like the rest of those runaways and misfits, she had held that money in her hands, never daring to think it was hers, or ever could be. He was god-like: all-seeing, omnipresent, vengeful.

Yes, she had sold drugs for him, and yes, she felt ashamed about it, but she had long ago forgiven herself for that downward spiral into which she fell when the life she ran to turned out to be far worse than the one she had fled.

And now it had happened again, yet another blow, and by far the worst. And to make it worse, Jesse's death was reminding her of what she had worked so hard to forget — that she was nothing, a nobody, that she had no control over anything, not even her own measly life. There was no escaping from her fate, not then, not now.

✦

Bailey sat at his desk, or rather, on the edge of it, a habit of his when he needed to be somewhere else instead of where he was meant to be; where he was paid to be. Apart from the requisite paperwork trails and updates, he didn't care to spend much time at the office, a kennel of clutter on the second floor of the station.

Being away from the workplace was conducive to sorting, solving and most importantly, deconstructing. Most of his analytic thinking was done in the car, or when he was being raced through an open park or field with the dogs, chariot-like, flanked on either side of him as he held tight to their leashes. Keeping up with their pace, understanding their desire to gallop on as he restrained them was the best workout ever.

The Collins lad was still on his mind, and a troubling, restless energy gnawed at him. Frankie hadn't been all that helpful, though Bailey suspected that he knew Collins; they must have moved in the same circles. He'd paid close attention to Frankie's expression when he'd shown him the post mortem photo of Collins's scarred back. Bailey had spared Frankie from seeing the more gruesome evidence on the young man's body, yet he was sure that he saw Frankie flinch before he changed the subject with that precise information for the drug bust.

The thing was, Bailey quite liked Frankie Harte. He was a good kid in a bad situation, like so many others – like Collins, sucked into a stinking underworld by circumstances.

Catching up on the voicemails from his desk phone, he listened to the disembodied message from the desk sergeant at Pearse Street, making notes as he heard the names of Beth Downes, Jesse Downes and Frankie, The Stump. At the same time, he picked up his mobile phone, buzzing now, a name flashing up on the screen: Roddy.

"About time!" he snapped. "Where are you? Didn't you get my messages?"

"Relax your kacks, dear!" replied a husky, effeminate tone, drenched in smoke. "Phone was off – no credit."

Bailey frowned. "How many times have I told you – if you need money just ask me, for Christ sakes!" he said, lowering his voice as he left his desk and made for the exit.

Roddy gave a throaty laugh. "Only you could be so kind and so angry in the same breath! How are you, Eric?"

Out on the street Bailey relaxed as he headed towards his car. "You need to come over soon – just so I have proof that you're actually still alive. The mother has been asking about you."

"Ah bless her and all the fermented grape juice," replied Roddy. "I will. I promise. Soon – or maybe Christmas. Now, what's up with you? What's on your mind?"

Bailey sighed. His prodigal brother, reduced to a voice on the other end of the phone, was the most infuriating person he knew. "I miss you, you prick! A bit of a fucking effort wouldn't hurt. Your sister is making another contribution to the human race, you know. I just heard – baby number five is on the way!"

"How lovely," Roddy responded, very quietly. There was a lengthy pause. "Congrats, Uncle. Give her my love, will you?"

Pay your family a visit and give it to her yourself, Bailey was tempted to retort. But he knew it was pointless. Roddy would never change, and as long as he was happy they'd have to make do with his absence. The odd phone call was better than nothing.

"Are you okay, Rod?" Bailey asked.

Another silence ensued before the breathy voice replied, "Are you?"

Now there was a question! "I'm working on this case. A dead kid – nineteen. He was one of your ménage."

"Tell it like it is, Eric. What was his name?"

"Collins, Sean. Murdered and dumped in a laneway this day last week. You hear anything? Roddy, are you still there?"

There was no answer, though Bailey could hear his brother's deep breathing.

"I suspect he knew something he was better off not knowing," Bailey went on. "Or that he crossed someone that he shouldn't have."

He heard Roddy clearing his throat.

"Where are you, Roddy, where are you hanging out these days?" Bailey asked, frustrated with the one-sided conversation.

"I have to go, bro. I'll be in touch."

The phone went dead.

Fuck.

Some detective he was, his mother would say yet again. How hard can it be to keep tabs on your own brother?

⅄

Mindless noise buzzed from the television as Beth, curled up in a ball on her sofa, stared blindly at it. At least she had begun to wash, hints taken from Luke's gift baskets of expensive toiletries – shampoo, body wash, lotions and potions she would never have dared sample, never mind buy for herself.

She hardly blinked or moved as Luke moved around the house, clearing, cleaning, stacking, storing until he appeared in front of her to block the pointless moving pictures from the screen with a bunch of opened letters in his hand.

"This cheque - I found, from your credit union. Ten grand, that's a lot of money?"

"Jesse's school fees, exam fees, sports fees. Completely forgot it was there."

Truth was, she didn't remember receiving it. Hadn't been checking her mail or paying bills. Tasks of little importance now.

"So do you want to return it?" he asked carefully. "There'll be interest accumulating on the loan. Maybe you don't need it now."

When she didn't respond, he tried another approach. "I could put it in the bank for you until you decide? Or you could blow it all on a trip away somewhere. A holiday might be just the thing."

He sounded so desperate to be helpful that she forced herself to smile. But that was all the encouragement he needed to wade in, all systems fired up.

"Forget the loan, Beth, I'll pay – and I can arrange everything. All you have to do is agree to come with me – South of France, Spain, Italy – wherever. I have good connections in the travel business. Could call in a favour and get us a nice place sorted. Somewhere to give you headspace. No strings, no obligation – just a place to breathe. What do you say?"

Breathe? Like that was a good thing. Every gulp, laborious and heavy through the leaden pain so constantly bearing down on her chest, on the vacant, twisting yearn of her womb.

"Jesse was ten pounds, two ounces when he was born. Did I ever tell you that? No, I don't suppose I did. I never talked about Jesse much – or anything else."

Luke reached out to embrace her. She made herself go limp, unresponsive to his touch.

"Does not talking about someone imply that you don't care? That they don't exist? That they don't matter? Twenty-two inches long, he was, and all the other mothers used to pop down to my hospital bed to ogle at the size of him. How could he have come from me, a pathetic squirt of a thing? And a massive head of hair he had too. He was the most gorgeous baby – a little cherub, straight out of a biblical painting. I never believed in God – the people who did always seemed to hurt me – but the day I found out I was pregnant, I learned to pray, and I prayed every day after that, that Jesse would be healthy, that he wouldn't – guess I asked for too much."

She sat forward, air gushing out of her with the pain, searing pressure to the back of her eyes. She could hear it now, as loud and clear as if she were there again, her quiet mewling while the security guard pounded on the locked door of the toilet cubicle, a used pregnancy test kit lying on the dirty floor at the feet of a skinny, shivering, teenage girl. Her greasy, lank hair covering her face, her scabby hands clasped in prayer as she had promised wholeheartedly that she would believe, if only God would promise that her child wouldn't end up like her.

"But the blood was in his veins," she mumbled.

🙶

If she had known then what she knew now, would she have done anything differently? Would she have dropped all the gear and stuffed those huge wads of notes – his profits – inside her pants and bra? Would she have sought out a chemist shop and purchased the pregnancy test from the boss man's ill-gotten gains? Would she have braved the disgust and suspicion of the shop assistants at the large department store as she scurried into the toilets to pee out that positive result?

It was a miracle that a little baby could thrive at all inside her pathetically undernourished teenage body, but thrive he did, his little heart pumping like a firecracker, changing everything.

It was a fucked-up start to a new life, that's for sure, but what irony that the man who had all but destroyed her had also given her the greatest gift of all. As that new life grew, it nourished her, giving her back her will to live, and with that second tiny heart beating for her, she found the strength to do something she never thought she could.

Inside that toilet, with the security guard pounding on the door and the grumbling queue of women waiting outside, that fifteen-year-old girl knelt down on the smelly floor and prayed, reaching for faith as she begged for strength and courage. She had to get away, from the drugs, and from the petty crime that financed them, but more importantly, she had to make sure that the boss man would never know this child.

⚔

The opposite of orderly, the entrance to the open access drug clinic swarmed with addicts as they waited for their prescription drugs, or a needle exchange, or therapy, or a miracle. Or maybe just some dinner.

Decked out in Jesse's oversized parka, Beth kept look-out from a safe distance, a thick woollen hat pulled down over her eyes and a scarf pulled up around her mouth. It wasn't long before Frankie appeared, shifty, agitated, the hood shrouding his wasted face. She watched him go inside as she stood firm and focused. Had done her homework, knowing the drill as she waited until he emerged again, his medicinal fix sorting him out for a couple of hours at least.

Frankie didn't hang around. Eyes down, shifty and nervous, he ignored offers from the more desperate heads wanting to sell or swap their maintenance for something stronger. He moved as swiftly as his lopsided body would allow, glancing over his shoulder every now and then. Keeping out of sight, she followed him through the city streets, back towards the now familiar haunt of the quays and away from the centre of everything, her heart pounding as all at once, there it loomed, the blood draining from her face at the sight of the crumbling, derelict flat complex.

Beth studied the blocks, a tomb to her degradation, the windows broken or boarded up, and she swallowed down a strange sound that gurgled at her throat – and the urge to run, and keep running away from this place. Regaining composure, her expression tightened as Frankie moved across the courtyard, a lone, pathetic figure in a broken-down playground. Waiting until he had disappeared inside, she took a deep breath and followed, listening at the foot of the stairs, hearing him climb higher as the reeking stench of human waste cloyed at her nostrils. Still she waited, until his footsteps ceased, and she heard a door open, but not close, and on a count of ten to calm her thumping heart, she found herself ascending. Slowly, cautiously, until she heard his footsteps once more, coming towards her now, and she squeezed her body tightly into a dark recess as he rushed past her. She waited, barely breathing until the sound of his footsteps ceased. Shuffling out again and up the last flight of stairs, she could see four doors, two completely boarded up, one broken down, revealing nothing but a wrecked shell of emptiness. The fourth door however, was open, a grim invitation to a cold and dimly lit hovel.

In one of its rooms she spied an unmade, dirty bed and her chest heaved with shallow gasps as she walked in the space, in and out of corners, touching the walls, the peeling wallpaper. Picking off a piece, big as her hand, she studied it, tracing the faded shape of a bird, a kingfisher, electric blue no longer, decades of neglect faded to grey. And she was transported, the grey altering to black abyss until light flooded the room and she was grabbed from behind and pushed violently to the ground.

"Word of advice!" Frankie snarled in her ear. "If you're gonna stalk someone around this filthy piss-pit, don't come here with your hair smelling of fucking roses!"

He loomed over her, fuming, a broken bottle in his raised hand. Beth raised her arms over her head, cowering, but just when she thought it might all end here and now, with jagged glass and pent-up rage, he stepped off, edgy as he put the bottle down to grab her once more, this time by the hood of her coat as he lifted her up, roughly pushing her towards the door. Beth resisted, fighting back as the two jostled, until she sensed that he was trying really hard not to hurt her. And took her chance.

"I've given your name to the police. Maybe you'll talk to them."

Frankie didn't look at all surprised. He brought his face close to hers; she could see close up the rot that had already set into his once perfect teeth.

"I don't give a bollix about the police, so fuck off!"

He shoved her out through the door and slammed it shut in her face.

Her first instinct was to shoulder her way back in, to plead with him to listen, but as she raised her fist to pound on the door, she saw the kingfisher wallpaper scrunched up tightly there, and in a nanosecond, she was spent of every ounce of fight her body had left.

That final night with Jesse's father, she had known she would crawl from his bed in the small hours of the morning, after he had taken the frustrations of the day out on her. And she would escape. She thought it almost funny that she survived these ordeals; they really ought to have killed her long ago. But she had learned to go outside of her own body, to elevate her spirit to another level. To be that other side of herself.

This last time was no different as she floated off to the safe space in her mind, where an overwhelming sense of imagined purity helped her to conjure all things newly born; a fresh budding rose, the scent of new grass that wafts in as the old is raked away, and the smell of a baby's skin. Her senses primed for survival. And as he hurt her with what he tended to describe as acts of love, she concentrated hard to stay there, in that otherness, oblivious to his mouth, sweet with whispered affections as his fingers crushed and stabbed at her flesh like blades. Addicted to her, in his own, unique and twisted way. His favourite vice - and she always had extra drugs to prove it. The only price he was willing to pay.

He understood her pain, he told her. He felt it too. Kindred spirits, they were, from the same tribe, the tribe of the neglected, the wounded.

She came back, that crazy bitch, her obsession fumbling with the faulty door handle of the hovel that Frankie had lately begun to call his new prison, a solitary confinement of his own making. He lashed out, this time with full force, grabbing her by the neck, and she fell compliant in his grip, without a struggle as he pinned her to the wall.

"You're a real fucking problem for me now, Lady!"

She was calm, too calm, and it rattled him.

"I need to ask you something," she said. "How come I didn't see it coming? How come I didn't know?"

As he tried to make sense of her, her eyes rolled back in their sockets so all he could see were the whites as she went limp. He let go of her and she slid to the floor. What the fuck was he supposed to do now? Give her a hiding until she forgot she ever saw him? Threaten to burn her fucking house down if she came near him again? Jesus, how fucking pathetic she looked, curled up at his feet.

He hated this – hated her for bringing this ridiculous situation to his doorstep. This shit he needed like a hole in the head. She unsettled him, too, with her need to know who was responsible for her son's death. Yet there was something familiar about this woman. It wasn't physical, or a memory; it was more of a feeling. And he fucking hated that.

When she regained consciousness, he was sitting on the floor opposite her, watching her, trying to figure out how he was going to get rid of her. But before she had even caught her breath, her mouth was off with the questions again.

"How can you live here? Why would you live here?"

"It's just a place to crash, and it's none of your business."

He deliberately kept a level of hostility in his tone, just to make sure she knew she couldn't hang around. She didn't seem fazed by him though and wasn't giving up, surprising him now with her knowledge of these buildings. Like the fact that the city council had been threatening to tear them down for the last twenty odd years, and that some big developer was after the land they stood on.

"It's a shithole," she went on. "This place was always a shithole. Should be bulldozed, instead of some vulture getting their claws in for low income rentals, easy money and the spiral of decay will continue. Poverty is big business. That's why it'll never go away."

"Are you okay to fuck off now?" he snapped. He was exasperated by her, especially now when she apologised, her eyes so intense that it felt like he'd been cut open.

"I know that you're not one of the bad guys, Frankie, and I'm also pretty sure now that you didn't give my son those bad drugs."

Fuck! Now what? Frankie didn't quite know how to respond to that, and in his awkwardness, as he played for time to respond, he found himself offering her one of his precious cigarettes.

Beth declined. "I gave up smoking when Jesse was born. Gave up a lot of things."

Frankie watched her, clenching and unclenching her fists. "A kid raising a kid, and so scared. Guess I had good cause. Guess I messed up."

"Lady, stop beating yourself up. You're not to blame. You could never compete with your son's addictions." Where the fuck that came from he wasn't sure. "That doesn't make you a bad mother," he blurted on, "and sorry, you won't want to hear it, but he made his own choices."

Frankie was still swallowing his surprise at the words that had just spewed out of his mouth when she suddenly rose up in front of him, getting into his face in wild, fiery anger.

"Fuck you!" she yelled. "My son knew better. He never would have done that to himself. I will make the scum who poisoned my son know what this pain feels like. You just watch me do it!"

Frankie scrambled to his feet, opened the door and made a sweeping gesture outwards. "You have to go now. I'm serious. I can't be dealing with this!"

Beth calmed herself, contrite now as she gathered what was left of her dignity and walked towards the door. Stopping before him, she recognized how he struggled to control his emotions and could see his growing fatigue, how his shoulders stooped, almost concave.

"I'm sorry," she said quietly, these parting words appealing to Frankie's better side.

"Look, Lady, it's not in me to rough up a woman, so I'm sorry too – about that." He was genuinely ashamed; drugs and fear did strange things to a person, but he hadn't lost all his humanity just yet. Frankie suddenly felt very vulnerable, and she knew it, she fucking knew it.

"Who are you hiding from?" she wanted to know.

He read her face, her body language, the tone in her voice, the softness in her gold-speckled eyes and he felt sure that her concern was genuine. He took in his surroundings.

"I'm not doing such a great job, am I?"

"I have a spare room," she said suddenly, surprising even herself with such a suggestion. No going back though, her gut was leading the madness.

Frankie raised his eyebrows, incredulous. "I could be a crazy bastard for all you know. Why would you want me in your home?"

"You could also be a kid in trouble, Frankie," she replied. "And I'd have no hesitation in bringing a kid in trouble into my home. You're wrecked and probably starving. And you need a good wash!"

"Jaysus, thanks for that." Suddenly conscious that he probably did smell like wet dog, he just stood there, dubious and indecisive as Beth started to back out of his filthy surroundings.

"Your call, Frankie."

⋏

Sometimes she would catch him watching her as she bathed, spying on her as she tended carefully to the bite marks, the bruises, and she knew that soon the gifts would appear. Pretty things – earrings, perfume, clothes, high-end trainers for the summer, boots for the winter – stuff she would inevitably sell to buy drugs, or barter for a better deal. The only thing she couldn't sell was the underwear – impracticable, flimsy nothings that she dared not get rid of, for he would order her to put them on before inevitably and savagely pulling them from her body in his twisted passion. She never let herself become attached to any of it, for it could just as quickly be snatched back for some transgression or mistake she didn't understand. And when that happened, she made sure she was as high as a kite before he got hold of her, for his punishments were always severe and always sexual.

For someone who had lifted his fists in brute force only once in his life, he was the most violent man she had ever met.

The last time they were together was different though, when she pretended to get high for what she hoped would be her final test of endurance with him. It wasn't about her anymore; even her junkie head knew better than to poison that little child inside her. Her blood was her child's blood; she was a warrior now, with something to fight for – her life no longer hers alone. So she had welcomed the pain of withdrawal, of cold fucking turkey, every nerve in her body craving heroin as the man who told her he was her saviour pummelled into her for the very last time. And waiting for sleep to overtake him, wiping herself clean, she had crawled away from that life, and from the father of her unborn angel.

⋏

Frankie sat at the kitchen table, devouring eggs and bacon like it was his last supper while Beth, perched on the edge of her chair, sipped her coffee and studied him.

"You scrub up well," she said.

"Thanks." He pointed to the sweater he was wearing. "And for this too – perfect fit."

Beth managed a weak smile. "Jesse never wore it. He always said I had crap taste in men's clothing."

"He was right," Frankie retorted giving her a cheeky glance. He was making short work of his meal. "There's a bit of an old man bang off it, but sure it's grand. I've already got the bushy boho beard. This could be the start of a new trend for me!"

Beth feigned shock. "Jesse was a smart ass too."

She fell silent then, still and watchful, until she noticed she was making Frankie uncomfortable and snapped out of it.

"What's going on with you, Frankie?" she asked.

"I'm not doing too good, as you can see. My legs are bollixed. I did a bad fix, injected heroin laced with wallpaper paste. Could've lost my leg. It's a miracle I didn't. Veins are fucked now though."

She really should gasp in shock and horror, vent her disgust that there were bastards out there who would do such a thing, but it would be pointless. She knew they existed and so did he.

"Why are you so afraid?" she persisted.

He stopped eating, and startled her as he pushed his chair back and stood away from the table, clutching his stomach and doubling over. Before she could react, he crouched on the floor on his hunkers, gasping, struggling to stand up, his body shaking uncontrollably. Her belly tightened as she watched him stagger from the kitchen to crawl up the stairs to the bathroom. Helplessly, Beth waited in the hallway, her hands clasped to her forehead, listening to him bring up the contents of his stomach over and over. When he finally reappeared, his eyes, rheumy and wet, were hooded with embarrassment.

"I'll take you to the clinic," was all that she said, grabbing her keys as Frankie locked his gaze on her.

As they left the house, neither of them noticed Luke's car coming around the corner.

⚶

Outside the blacked-out windows of the clinic, Beth's car idled on double yellow lines, traffic honking for her to move on. Frankie got out, shutting the passenger door to hobble around and lean weakly in through the driver's window, "Thanks for everything, Lady. Now go home. This is no place for you to be. We're all square now."

"I'll find a parking space. Won't be too far from here." She looked straight ahead, a stubborn side profile that was intended to warn him not to argue. He didn't have the luxury of time to argue, she reasoned, needed all his energy for the persuasive begging he would have to engage in now to get an unscheduled shot of the maintenance.

As he moved off with a grunt of resignation, Beth found a safer spot to park from where she could still keep an eye on the door to the clinic. Catching movement in her wing mirror, she froze, infuriated at the sight of Luke, suddenly there now, at her window, tapping it with his knuckle.

Cursing under her breath, she reluctantly wound it down.

"Don't get mad, Beth. I'm worried," Luke protested, his brow furrowed. "What are you doing here, with that guy?"

"What are *you* doing here?" she snapped, seething now. "Are you checking up on me? How dare you!"

She deliberately avoided looking at him, like a bold child caught in the act. He didn't move away though.

Keeping her eye on the clinic entrance, she softened her tone. "Luke, it's all right – really. This is just something I have to do. I'll explain later. Now, please go. I'm just helping this kid out, and I don't want to scare him away. Please?"

She sighed with relief as he silently backed off and returned to his car, which she could now see had been parked a couple of spaces behind her. "I'll phone you!", she called after him, just as Frankie emerged from the clinic.

As Beth was about to call out to him, her attention was drawn to another man, hard-headed menace emanating from him as she saw him walk swiftly up to Frankie, who suddenly broke into a run. Panic engulfed her as she saw the man easily overpower Frankie and repeatedly punch him, and she watched helplessly as Frankie fell to the ground to take the relentless pounding of blows without any effort to defend himself.

Suddenly, from deep in Beth's belly a harrowing scream emerged and with both hands she put all her weight on the car horn, the sound blaring out in unison with her own banshee screech. The man looked up in her direction, the momentary distraction allowing Frankie to squirm out of his grip and land his attacker and well-placed kick to the balls.

Frankie scrambled to his feet and ran for his life towards Beth's car.

"Go! Move it! Move it, for fuck's sake!" he screamed, jumping into the passenger seat as Beth pulled out into the traffic, drivers behind her standing on brakes and honking horns.

She could see the thug, his fat triangular neck strained and purple as he galloped after them, and her eyes danced between the road ahead of her and the scene behind. She caught sight of another car pull up beside Frankie's pursuer, who jumped into it.

"They're still following us," she said, her tone strangely calm, slamming on the accelerator to swerve down a one-way street, dodging an oncoming car before racing into a T-junction where she cut across traffic on a main road. Frankie could hardly breathe, his hands pressed into the dashboard, his eyes wide and incredulous as he stared at her. Beth put her foot to the floor until she was sure she had lost their pursuers and only then, did she ease up on her speed to find a route home. Neither uttered a sound for the remainder of the journey.

⅄

The universe listened to a junkie hooker, a parasitical boil on the arse of society, unclean, but somehow, gifted with this new, inner strength that would allow me to bare my face to the world. Shoving my timid and beaten-down self out of the shade to reveal the guts I needed to flee, yet again, and be reborn. Just like before, when I ran from my violent mother, it wasn't easy now to flee from the tormentor that replaced her. To get out from under that gaze, a gaze that loathed and desired me in equal measures, gorging on my innocence, and afterwards, hating me for it. And I was risking my life, of this, I had no doubt. I had learned his way of dealing with the people who fell into his lair. How he controlled them with a flash of his sharp gaze, giving his orders without even raising his voice, and they knew too. Knew that if they failed him, disappointed him, they'd probably end up weighted at the bottom of the canal, dumped in a sodden boggy grave or buried deep in a hidden fissure of a mountainside. Ironically, I understood that he did what he did to cement his reputation with the hardened criminals that didn't even know him yet, but would find out, and to their peril if they crossed him. The power of his suggestion was enough; the power of his command was all it took. And all the while he had that way about him, wore such a veneer of respectability that most people wouldn't even believe it if they heard just what a sick fuck he really was. All this I had learned, and tried to forget now as I made my plans, forcing to the back of my brain that my child's eyes were his. That's the thing with beauty, isn't it? How it blinds you to the reality of what's really going on beneath the surface.

Chewing on her bitten nails, Beth watched Frankie from the kitchen window as he paced back and forth in her small back yard. Sometimes she glimpsed Jesse there, sprawled out on the wooden bench he had helped her assemble when he was nine, when he was sweet and gentle and full of joyful jabber. They had painted that bench a different colour each year, the rainbow spectrum revealed in its now flaking paint. Now there was another boy, pensive, frightened, with fresh, angry bruises glaring at her as she stepped outside to offer him a mug of sweet tea. He tried to take it in his right hand, forgetting for an instant as it wobbled and spilled in his trembling, unbandaged paw.

Beth brushed loose flakes of water-meadow green top-coat from the bench and sat down, Frankie filling the space beside her, sipping carefully from his tea and smoking his last cigarette.

"I lost drugs that belonged to a mad fucker. Calls himself The Poet. Actually, someone else stole them off me, but in the game I'm responsible."

He rested his hand, limp and useless, on his knee and examined it closely, the raw red ridges like rope marks between the stumps where he still could feel his fingers.

"Uncut, it was worth about a thousand, but once cut and bagged, it would have been worth four times that amount, and he keeps doubling it for every week I don't pay it back. I've lost count now, have no idea how much I'm in for." Frankie gave a sudden involuntary shiver. "I tried to sell more gear to pay off the debt, and got done for possession. The cops have confiscated it. Do you have any tablets – painkillers?"

"I don't know, Frankie. I generally don't keep anything like that here."

"I'm not freaking out on you. This is what happens from coming off the gear."

Instinctively, Beth reached out to comfort him, but he flinched and ducked away from her touch.

"Please? Something – anything to take the edge off the pain."

She recalled a time when Jesse had been up all night with a toothache, a wisdom tooth that was later removed, and she'd had to find a pharmacy in the middle of the night. She rushed now to the kitchen to rummage through drawers and found a half-used tinfoil pack of soluble aspirin, well past their sell-by date but probably okay. Better than nothing.

Back in the kitchen, while she filled a glass of water from the tap, she noticed the credit union cheque on the counter top where Luke had left it: ten thousand euro. She looked into the back yard. Frankie was no longer there. Her heart lurched a little until she found him again, in her tiny sitting room – the good room – fidgeting, restless; she knew the tingling in his veins was driving him crazy. He was standing in front of her wall of photographs, and she followed the line of his sight to the image he was looking at.

"That's what I've been meaning to explain to you about," she said, offering him the aspirin and water. "About my Jesse."

Frankie didn't react, though the look on his face alerted Beth to trouble, more trouble, just as the doorbell shrieked. Startled once more, he rushed to the front window, peeping out through Beth's dollhouse net curtains.

"It's that dick, Bailey!" he snapped. "What the fuck is he doing here? Did you call him?"

Puzzled, she moved to the window to see a suited man, a stranger. "I don't know him," she said. "Who is he?"

Frankie was already at the back door. "Stall him. I'm done talking to cops!"

Panic surged through her as he disappeared over her backyard wall, and the bell kept ringing, over and over.

Composing herself, she opened her front door and faced the policeman, courteous as he held out his badge to introduce himself. She remembered her conversation with the desk sergeant; so he had passed on her message after all! Beth glanced at the badge, deliberately slow as she did what she was told, stalling time for Frankie.

"A bit late, aren't you?" she snapped as he invited himself inside.

"Not sure I understand what you mean by that?" Bailey responded, vigilant in his scrutiny. "You are Mrs Downes?"

"Miss Downes – single mother."

She led him into the sitting room. No view of the back yard, where she hoped Frankie was well hidden, but not gone.

"I understand you've been making enquiries about your son's death," Bailey said. "And please accept my apologies for not responding sooner. I appreciate your patience, under the circumstances … and I'm very sorry for your loss."

"Really?" She couldn't keep the sarcasm out of her voice. "So you've read his file?"

Bailey nodded and looked down at her, maintaining eye contact. She knew that gaze only too well, his presence invading her space, crowding the room, irritating her. She took a step back.

"Then you understand, Detective, that I have no answers for you – only questions."

"We're not giving up on the investigation of your son's death, I can assure you of that." He noticed the wall of photographs of Jesse and without taking his eyes off them, he went on: "We have spoken to his friends at school and to witnesses who were at the club that night, but none of them seem to know the source of the drug that Jesse took. Any new information might just help us move forward."

Beth perched on the arm of the sofa, fiddling with a hand-painted wooden coaster, the intricate pattern of a mandala. "From his own gifted hand," she said. "Jesse made this for me, only a couple of years ago. I must have mentioned sometime that I quite liked those patterns, how they meant something to the individual who created them, how staring into the lines and circles brought me to focus on what was important, brought me balance. He was listening, that day. And he made me one. I thought I knew him then, who he could have been."

She angrily spun the coaster on to the floor. Bailey picked it up and set it respectfully on the coffee table. In the awkward silence, his eyes returned to the wall of images.

"There's a young man I'm interested in talking to – Frankie Harte. Do you know him?"

Beth glanced first at him and then at the door, hoping that Frankie had fled after all. "If you know about my son, you obviously know about my interest in Frankie or you wouldn't be asking."

"I am trying to help, Miss Downes. The station received a call from a concerned friend of yours – Luke Thompson? Something about an altercation today at Riverside Drug Clinic."

She jumped to her feet, defiant. So Luke had seen everything.

"Mr Thompson had no right to call you. Anyhow, he's got it all wrong. I spoke to a young man there about Jesse. But so what! I was fed up waiting for you lot to do something!"

"I must caution you, Miss Downes. You shouldn't interfere with police business," Bailey said. "It's not wise for you to go looking for or to question drug dealers, even the petty ones. They're dangerous individuals. Let us do our job."

Beth folded her arms across her chest and scowled at him.

"One last question," Bailey said. "Are you acquainted with Byron Frazer?"

Beth's arms fell away from her chest, her defensive stance disabled as she inhaled sharply at the sound of that name, a name she mouthed now, every syllable suctioning vital air from her lungs. "Why … why should I know him?"

"That's his daughter there" – Bailey pointed at a photograph on the wall – "Rebecca Frazer… with your son."

Beth could feel him watching her as she followed his eye to the photograph of the girl with the dip-dyed hair.

ᐱ

Her stomach empty now, and bile burning up into her gullet, she stood very still, her two hands on either side of the hole that Jesse had thumped out of the wall on the night that he died. Beth rested her clammy forehead over it, hearing the echoes of him screaming at her, reliving it as if it was happening all over again. Too much to bear, this new truth, every turn of her day pulling her deeper and deeper into this nightmare.

Sluggishly tearing herself away, she went into her bedroom and sat on the edge of the bed, examining the crumpled piece of wallpaper from Frankie's flat. The faded kingfisher, staring out at her, a length of time that stood still until she snapped back, returning it carefully to the bedside locker, where she could keep it in her sight.

Listless, she kicked off her flip-flops and felt something under her foot, sticking out from under her bed. Beth knelt down and picked up an empty plastic packet, the green powdery traces still visible, and at once, she knew for sure what had been plaguing her, tormenting her, her face creased up in pain.

Together, she and I, sank to the floor, curling up into our place of safety, the foetal arc of our body the only way we can deal with our agony; and I feel sorry for her - only her, as every ounce of sorrow drains from her.

She longs to peel her skin back, to shed it. To ease this excruciating pain. But she is afraid, for underneath she'll find me. She knows now that I am there, and how I can help her now.

Rebecca lurked at the bottom of her own garden, a nymph-like beauty with a monster appetite, scanning hawk-like her surroundings before she entered the half-lit gazebo. Inside, it was an Aladdin's cave filled with all the luxury that Pop's money could provide – cut glass lanterns, expensive Scandinavian furniture, cashmere throws and pillows, a stacked drinks cabinet. Her mother's drinking den.

She kept glancing up towards the house. There was a light glowing from the master bedroom where Mammy probably lay comatose right now. Rebecca didn't drink. She didn't need to. Besides, alcohol pickled your face, and she didn't want to end up looking like that lush, a wrinkled old cunt at fifty.

She plopped down on one of the plush chairs and took a wrap of cocaine from her pocket. She needed it right now. She'd been having flashbacks – that stupid fucker with the phone, his eyes gaping out at her through the clear plastic bag as it sucked in and out of his mouth, in and out, in and out, an eternity until it ceased. But those eyes, those fucking eyes, staring out at her. She had to make them go away.

As she took her first snort, she was rocked forward on to her feet by a voice from the darkness.

"Knew I'd catch you down here if I waited long enough. How's it all going these days, Becca baby?"

Frankie Harte moved into the soft light, a halo forming around his beaten, cut-up face.

"Thought you were still locked up?" she quipped, swallowing hard, barely able to look at him. She sat back again, faking composure until her brain settled and her natural fierceness returned.

"Like clockwork, down the back garden for your nightly fix after Mammy dearest has drunk herself into a coma. Feeling good now, Becca? Going clubbing? Or are you off to get hooked?"

As he moved closer, she jumped up, grabbed her phone and moved round behind the seat.

"You better get out of here, Frankie, before someone comes."

"Go on, call your lackeys over, baby girl," he said. "Sure I'll be done before their mammies even have their shoelaces tied."

Rebecca lowered her voice. "What do you want, Frankie? Money? I can get you a couple of grand from the house. Just give me a minute."

"Your daddy's dirty, poxy bloodstained money? No thanks."

He yanked away the chair between them and pushed it across the gazebo, reaching out to touch her perfect face with his mutilated hand. She flinched and a little scream escaped from her as she knocked his hand away, repulsed.

"It's over," she said. "We're finished."

He laughed harshly, bitterly as he remembered how she once had welcomed his touch, opening her legs for him any time he needed her. "Do you ever think about what we used to get up to, the stuff we used to do, right here, in Pop's back yard – right under his fucking nose?"

"Frankie, I'm sorry about what happened to you. Really, if I could settle it I would."

"Couldn't possibly have him catching his precious with a load of his blow up her nose and bags of grenades down her deep, deep pockets, now could we? The drugs you stole from him to give away like sweeties to your mates – did you party with them while Pops got off on torturing your stupid, gullible fella? But he didn't know I was your fella, now did he? Riding his precious doll, night after night." Frankie pulled her roughly towards him. "Before you fucked me up. And I know all about Jesse, that bloke you were seeing, the one you had me pass the gear on to. What a job you did on him! Good-looking bastard, though not so smart." He whispered into her ear, "That mother of his – Jesus! Completely bonkers, you know. Relentless, she is. I wonder what she'd do if she knew that it was you who gave Jesse the pills that killed him. I wonder what your daddy would do if he knew it was you bringing all this heat on him."

Rebecca gulped. "What do you want from me?"

"Nothing, I want nothing. Not from you, you sad fuckin' bitch. I just came for one thing."

Suddenly he was on her, yanking her head back by the hair, gripping her chin with his mutilated hand and forcing her lips apart with his tongue. She dug her nails into his neck and shrieked her muted disgust.

Just as suddenly Frankie let her go, wiping his mouth with the back of his hand and spitting at her, a thick marbled glob of blood and phlegm landing on her face and dripping slowly down on to her expensive leather pumps.

"I forgive you." Was all that Frankie said as he turned and walked back into the black night.

From the back door, Beth had called out to him and almost said his name, Jesse's, but stopped herself, just in time. When only the silence returned, she paced the floor, thoughts drilling around her brain until she felt her forehead bulge with the pressure and she moved upstairs. Stopping dead, her limbs froze. There, taped over the hole that Jesse had punched through the landing wall, was the piece of kingfisher wallpaper. Her arms and legs a leaden weight, she reached for it, peeling it carefully from the wall to turn it over. *You'll find what you need at The White Lady. Refrain from belligerence*, it read.

In the dim light, Beth fell on her knees, crawling on the floor towards her bedroom as she sobbed out her fear, her frustration, her sense of abandonment. Frankie had come back, had been here during the scant hours when she had lain slumped on her sofa, passed out with exhaustion and into her nightmares. Now she noticed the contents of her handbag, scattered on her bed, her purse open and empty. She was not surprised. She could not be angry, but her sense of foreboding shivered over her, and she grabbed her coat to run to him.

When she reached the flats, abandoning her car to the wasteland as she entered the dregs of that building, she knew what she would find, how she would find him – Frankie, his eyes glazed over, still warm as the needle fell from his arm and onto the dirty floor. As he took his last breath, his body slumped forward and into her arms, she shook him and slapped his face until finally, she succumbed to the truth of this ghost of a boy having given in, given up. Cradling him in her arms, Beth's sobs echoed throughout the dereliction as hours later, Bailey found her there.

Responding to her agonizing call, and keeping a respect-ful distance, he waited, and waited, as time stood still, and he called it in, requesting an ambulance as he gently prised her away from Frankie Harte's lifeless corpse.

LADY

I learned so much from my ghost child, Frankie. The gaps in my history with Byron Frazer, stuff only rumoured but never proven. The poor wretch, found dehydrated and starving at eleven years of age, curled into his mother's rotten corpse, only discovered there when entwined with the musical, tinny strains of a transistor radio, the neighbours had become suspicious of the strange low howling that was emanating through the thin walls of the flats.

Had they heard the screams of his mother as she was beaten to death? Probably, but people don't interfere in domestics, now do they.

He'd been taken into care until he was sixteen, foster family to foster family, so hardly surprising what emerged back out into the world, or the consequences when the shit hit the fan. When the emperor seized his crown of pain. It took him two years to track down his father, and he gave as good as the old man had doled out to his long suffering wife. And when Byron had finished his father off, he'd walked straight to the nearest police station. He did twelve years, reading, studying, watching and growing, and Byron Frazer left prison a highly educated, yet twisted man with a reputation that instilled fear and loathing. If you can kill your own da and still sleep like the dead, you must be a destroyer. And so his reputation grew, and according to my ghost child, was still growing, omnipotent, all-seeing, pure evil.

Funny how what goes around comes around. Entering those stinking flats again, the feeling of it all. The same smell of piss on concrete, the same eerie echo of things crawling about unknown. The ghosts, the essence of lingering misery, the smell of death, and the same knots twisting my gut, the same grey light, the same fucking wallpaper!

Frankie almost beat me up once, but you know that already – held a broken bottle over my head. I think I almost welcomed death then, but the old me was begging for mercy, and I saw what flashed across his dark expression. A knowing, an instinct that people like us have about each other. And he gave me something so precious, something that no-one, not even my own son, had given me. He gave me his time, and he listened to my madness and my grief, and I will love him forever for letting me spew it all out. And for understanding. The anger that had welled up inside me, the frustration, the madness that had me grinding my teeth until my gums swelled and my jaw ached.

So I had taken him home. It's funny now to think of his awkwardness in my space, all limping, lanky limbs, clumsy with his missing fingers, and sick, so very sick, tiptoeing around my stuff, hardly daring to touch any of it. My heart had gone out to him because I knew what was going through his head. *Would the DVD player be enough for his next fix? How much would he get for the meagre contents of that jewellery box?* He had taken money from my purse, but he could've had it all – everything I owned. I wouldn't have cared.

Frankie harboured more demons than I dared let myself think about, the pressure coming from all sides, his spirit snapped. Because of it, he broke the cardinal rule: he turned tout. And sentenced himself to death.

In my dreams I still cradle him in my arms, whispering in his ear that I forgive him, that I'd known all along he'd supplied the drugs that killed my son; that I never blamed *him* for it; that I was after the big fish and he was bringing me closer.

I still imagine his final moments, setting up his fix, weeping (for there were still tears on his face when I found him). How I wish I had collected them. Preserved them. Licked them dry. And I see him, as I've seen myself, pinching skin in preparation for the final puncture, the failed attempts until finally, in the crook of his arm, he finds a place not yet too damaged to take the needle, his back against the wall, hunched over, waiting for the misery to end.

And I swear, I saw peace on his face when I kissed him goodbye.

Now I feign sleep as that good man, Luke, keeps coming back, sharing my bed, holding me at night, sleeping like a baby after I've faked it. I'm good at that.

He got me what I needed – super strength sleeping pills and Valium, enough to dull the pain after that nice detective brought me home, all caring and concerned. Now *he's* a man I could like – in another life.

The pills don't always work, though I do sometimes get a nice respite from reality. But not the morning after Frankie's death when I woke to the sound of scraping, or was it digging, and I thought I was in a dark place, immobile and cold, with wet dirt falling on my face. I lay there for a while, trying to figure out what the sound was, was it real or imagined, and where it was coming from. Until it screamed for my attention and I staggered out to the landing to find Luke carefully plastering over Jesse's hole in the wall.

Covering over Jesse's heart.

I rushed at him, punching him, shoving him out of the way, and clawed at the fresh plaster until the hole reappeared. And I fucking lost it, spilling out hysterical vitriol, my bitter, twisted soul filled with hate for everything.

And all the while Luke waited, arms outstretched, pleading for my forgiveness.

My forgiveness. The fool! Why wouldn't he give up on me?

The hole restored, I heard my son's heart beat once more, the same sore rhythm as mine. I let Luke kiss me, so compliant to his touch. Old habits die hard. I am resigned, for I know now for sure, that once I am done, he will be rejected. My knight in shining armour, if ever I was looking for one. Sweet man, with his slim, gentle fingers and schoolboy hair, flopping across kind eyes, hiding the hurt of rejection despite my unwavering indifference.

I have used him.

He asked me once why I never looked at him. I didn't understand the question. In hindsight, I know exactly what he meant. The look that he reflected back at me, the look that told me his body and soul ached for me. The way, I imagine now, my son had looked at her, Rebecca.

A look that I am incapable of giving to any man.

Is it normal for a mother to love her son so much that it is enough? That she doesn't ever crave the touch of a lover? And anyway, what did I know about sex and love, when my only experience was to be controlled by a man only in love with death?

If you look up narcissism, low and behold, there he is, Byron. The world outside of his own does not scare him. It is inferior, not good enough, because in his own eye, he is the world. Same goes for anyone close to him, anyone he sees as a reflection of himself.

The ones he calls *his*. It is not love. It is possession.

Getting rid of Luke is the only thing to do. Going to the bank and cashing that credit union cheque is the only thing to do. Getting into Byron Frazer's fucking club is the only thing to do. And she, my helpless other self, with her relentless clawing for her ghosts, won't stop me.

⅄

You could be one of the thousands who pass by The White Lady every day or night, completely unaware of its existence, a discreet venue with nothing but a tiny brass plaque on the wall with the initials "W. L." embossed in neat black lettering. It is the task of just one bouncer, bloated with steroids, to guard the heavily reinforced door, a pack of thugs only moments away should there be any trouble. Access is granted only to the chosen ones, and once inside, patrons devour the pleasures only hinted at in the double entendre one-liner speech bubbles on the posters advertising the star attractions.

Shadowed beneath a large umbrella, dressed in the prettiest clothes I own, hair and make-up all done, I wait and wait until, finally, the plush car pulls up, his henchman, Hatch, opens the rear passenger door, and there he is in all his finery: the boss man; the father killer.

The narcissist. The Poet.

All I can do is stare, and stare, the air sucked out of my lungs, my scalp tightening as however safe in the shadows, the closeness of him pumps dread from my heart to my head. Fight or flight, either way I'm fucked, and I swallow hard as the still handsome bastard enters the club, his club, and I follow, brazen on the outside, rattling on the inside, to mingle in behind his entourage and eclectic punters.

The hostess comes out of her caged booth, all decked out in her brash tuxedo, boobs pushed up, cheap perfume hanging heavily in the dead air around her. The slag checks my coat and umbrella, assuming I'm one of his thug's whores, and as Byron and his gang disappear into a faux art deco elevator, all gold and ivory paint, I move quickly from the foyer to the Ladies room where I wait for the show to begin. I giggle with nerves at this movie scene moment, a classic hold of tension until I hear the music begin, and I stroll out, chin up as I head towards the lounge. I get myself an overpriced gin and tonic because what the fuck are people drinking these days anyway, and I place my clenched ass on a stool at the end of the bar to watch the comings and goings, rejecting the inevitable filthy fucks who assume I'm looking for a ride. *Whatever dudes,* my attention remains fixed and interested on the several waitresses that move around in high heels and tightly trussed-up costumes, and the filthy heckling fucks make of that what they will.

While I watch and listen and I sip my drink, and it isn't too bad. Not bad at all.

⚔

Bailey woke up with a splitting headache and cringed at the annoying hum of his phone on the pillow beside him. He'd finished off a bottle of wine last night, and one the night before. Frankie's death should not have rattled him. His death was inevitable; and better by his own hand than that of his persecutor. But still, Bailey couldn't get the poor kid out of his mind.

What a waste! What a mess. Was he to blame – putting pressure on the kid to give him something on The Poet? And would there be a funeral to send him off? There was nothing on his record about next-of-kin. He'd have to make some enquiries about that. Maybe Beth Downes would know. That lady – so much more to her than grief and beauty. He should talk to her again.

The phone began humming once more. This time Bailey answered it.

"I've counted seven missed calls to you, Eric. Is everything all right?"

Bailey sat up and got out of bed. "Roddy! Sorry, I slept in. You okay?"

"Are *you*? It's not like you to sleep late. Are you alone?"

Bailey laughed. "What are you now, acting as agent for Mother? What's up bro? Roddy?"

"That boy, Collins, lord rest him."

"Go on." Bailey was on the move now, professional detective once again as he slid into his jeans and made his way to the kitchen. Two shots of espresso and toast for soakage would sort him out.

"He was hanging out with a girl called Rebecca, Rebecca Frazer," Roddy said and paused. Bailey imagined his brother's thin, pale fingers bringing a cigarette to his fleshy mouth. "Do you know her, Eric?"

"Yeah, unfortunately. Just scraped another of her acquaintances off a dirty floor."

"Ah, no!" Roddy cried. "Who was it this time, for chrissakes?"

"Lad called Frankie Harte – same age as Collins. He knew our little friend Rebecca too."

"I'm sorry to hear that, Eric. Too much of this now."

"Could you do me a favour, Roddy? Could you meet me? Just so I can see you in the flesh and know that you're okay."

"Go on, you! Big softie! I'm doing fine. And you've enough on your plate with that woeful job of yours. Why anyone in their right mind would want to get into police work, I'll never know."

"I'm not in my right mind, so there's that. And you're changing the subject, you prick!" The espresso was kicking in, life returning to the bleakness of normal. "I mean it,

Roddy, the very fact that you know these kids is alarming to me. How so? And where the fuck are you?"

"Eric, really. I am where I want to be, where Roddy can hide and I can be me." He almost sang the sentence. Roddy had always been a good singer. "I'm also in a place where I can keep my ears open – and I will, Eric, for you and for two dead kids. I'll call you soon, promise."

⅄

We went shopping, and for the first time in her life, no expense was spared. I had a ball; she, however, cringed every step of the way. And once back at her place, as she emptied the contents of the designer-label shopping bags on to her bed, my mouth watered at the jewelled luxury of the pretty lace and satin corsets. Inspired by my gin-fuelled reconnaissance at The White Lady, ruby red and emerald green fabrics, tumbling out like silken, precious gems, stockings silkily slipping through my fingers.

And then she faced me for the first time in front of a mirror.

Casting off her nunnery-white underwear, I swear I caught her checking out her reflection, admiring it, our nakedness, our lovely smoothness. There had been some advantage to her clean living after all. She is fine. Her skin, smooth, supple and, except for that ghastly self-imposed burn on her hand, unblemished; no sun exposure, her scars faded to oblivion. Her breasts pert, her bottom plump and round, her slim hips curving delightfully into her narrow waist.

And it happened, finally, as she slid the emerald fabric over her breasts, the cool satin caressing her skin, a sigh escaped from her, or perhaps it was from me, and I was fierce as she succumbed, practicing my sexiest poses in those high-heeled stilettos, getting my balance right, dressing for sin. And I showed her what pleasure feels like. What it should have felt like all along. How to feel it, to be it. How to be it to feel it, and when she is done with her weeping, and we are one, I paint my face, for only that other face will do now as we go together, back to the hell from which we came.

⚑

Getting past the security guard for a second time required a little more effort in summoning up my best brazen hussy and the flash of a big smile at the square-headed security guard giving me the once-over. Gay or straight, it's hard to tell. So I play the friendly *how are you* with some direct eye contact, as if I know him and know the drill, and I was alone so what harm could I possibly do? My brass neck gets me in, and I just keep smiling as he holds the door for me and I ask him where the manager is and he directs me to her. The grand dame in charge.

Now she's another story. Mags, on the far side of desirable with her orange fake tan and pumped lips, sizing me up enviously.

"We don't take on staff without a recommendation. Who sent you here?"

"I know Mr Frazer. From the old days."

"Oh you do, do you? How so?"

The question lingers as Mags stares at me through her false spidery eyelashes.

"He wouldn't appreciate you asking," I say.

Her bitchy attitude shifts visibly. She might give me a shot, she says, even though Mr Frazer didn't mention sending anyone. "But he'll be in later anyway, so if there's going to be a problem—"

"There won't be a problem," I assure her, staring her down as she hovers indecisively. "I just want to earn a living. Serve drinks, nothing more."

She's wavering. She knows the deal with Byron and what could happen if she gets this wrong. So just in case, she beckons me to follow her through the empty club, all its grubby business laid bare in the full glare of the lights.

"Most of our girls are eastern European, and they're not staying long these days, so we might have a temp slot for you."

Once she has me in the back room, Mags reassumes her superior attitude and orders me to strip. I play along, fumbling with my coat, being all coy and modest, lifting my dress over my head. I can see her twitch with resentment as I stand there, expressionless in my lovely new underwear. I look good. I know it. I feel it. She knows it, though she pretends not to. She nods in a way that tells me she regards me as nothing special, but I know I have her approval. I hurriedly put my dress back on and follow her out again.

"I'll give you a slot for tonight, and bring your own costume," she barks as I move past her. The smug bitch puts her arm across the door and blocks me from leaving. "There are a few things to remember while working at The White Lady. The tips are generous if you play your cards right. Your mouth stays shut at all times, blinkers on. And make sure you have a bit of fun with the feelers – the skulls are paying well for the privilege."

"Of course," I say, nodding my head mechanically. As I exit, Mags is barking again, one last dig to put me in my place. "And don't assume you're in yet. Personally, I think you're too old. I doubt if the skulls will go for you. But we'll let the boss man decide. You can be sure that I'll be letting Mr Frazer know about you."

That's the plan, Bitch! I'm smiling all the way out of that fucking club, muttering under my breath, *let the boss man decide.*

⚓

That kid – Collins. I know what happened to him.

Bailey reread the text before hitting his brother's number. "Rod? What the fuck?"

The voice was low, melancholic. "He had the most beautiful eyes, though I only admired them from afar. Too young for me, you understand, an ageing motherfucker fag in a dress, but I could fantasise, couldn't I. That's what being human is really, isn't it – desire?"

"Roddy? Why didn't you tell me this before?"

"I saw him in clubs, in pubs, at private parties where old bent codgers salivated at the thought of owning his cute tight arse."

As Roddy's voice trailed off, Bailey unclenched the phone, the imprint of it white on the palm of his hand.

"You're fucking stoned, Roddy, you prick!"

"Sticks and stones, it is what it is."

Bailey could hear what he imagined to be his brother's clunky arm jewellery rattling, and the long, drawn-out silence of a joint slowly inhaled. Was he crying?

"What happened to him, Roddy?"

"He was born. He was different. He ran away. He sought to fit in. He found his tribe."

"Just like you, brother?"

"Just like me, Eric. Except I, being far from brave, have stayed in my place. Here in the underground. Kids these days, they won't accept that fine line. They want it all – and fair fucks to them, they should have it. But if you dabble, if you play the hard game, you better know that it will end, and end badly."

"The post mortem didn't show any drugs on this one, Roddy. Where are you going with all of this?"

"It's not about drugs, not this time."

Bailey heard a sob, followed by another infuriating silence. He was getting impatient. "Tell me what happened to Collins."

"I let him stay with me, all platonic, as was his wish. But he told me things, about fitting in and about how he got his kicks. You think you know, Mister Lawman? You don't."

Roddy's voice trailed off again and Bailey held his tongue, waiting as the heat rose in his blood.

"Those beautiful eyes saw too much, knew too much, and so they had to go."

The phone went dead. Bailey almost threw up. He hadn't told his brother how Collins died.

✦

My first night on and the burlesque show is in full flow, as am I, swinging these magnificent hips in my ruby costume, moving from table to table like a pro, taking orders, dodging groping hands. My feet hurt, so I lean against the bar and remove a stiletto to rub the ache, pain etched on my face as a voice like dulcet cello strings whispers in my ear.

"You'll get used to it."

I turn around and find her there, Miss Subrosa, star of the show, sipping from a cocktail and smiling down at me. A favourite with the punters, she had just come off stage, her blue-black wig flapping around a smooth, angular face, lace blouse clinging to skinny arms, and long, long legs poured into black-and-white striped leggings. And those crazy cat eyes, hollowed out with thick kohl, lips full-on rouge for her best Liza-with-a-z routine; so beautiful, so fragile.

"You're good though. I haven't seen anyone navigate the vultures with such skill for a long time. It's been quite a joy to behold."

"You're Miss Subrosa?" I ask as innocently as I can muster while I shove my now swollen foot back inside the un-yielding shoe.

She opens out her finger-bejewelled gloved hands with an air of drama. "At your service, pretty lady."

I like her already and can't help but feel grateful for the friendly face. "Is it really that obvious, my contempt for the punters?"

Subrosa laughs, a big, generous throaty roar. "And who could blame you, my darling. But I do need to offer you a word of advice, if you don't mind. For your own sake, play the game. Give a little and keep the boss happy. He likes to keep an eye on his money-makers."

Our budding friendship is rudely interrupted by Mags, hands on hips wafting along in a cloud of hairspray and nylon static.

"Boss wants to see you," she snaps at Subrosa. She turns to me. "And you're not getting paid to hold up the bar, so get back to it."

As Mags walks away, Subrosa follows her, mimicking her big-ass swagger and turning back to make a funny face at me. I watch them disappear through a door covered by a heavy velvet curtain and of course I follow them, discreetly as I can. They disappear into a carpeted hallway that leads all the way to a storeroom at the back of the club and I peep through a crack in the door, barely breathing.

And there he is in all his close-up, fucked-up glory, better looking than I remembered, the grey hair lending him an air of distinguished elegance. He is leaning against the wall, smoking a cigarette while one of his thugs slams Subrosa down hard over a table.

Instantly I'm right back there, in that terror.

"I swear I don't know!" she pleads and I stick my fist in my mouth to stop me from yelling out.

Byron Frazer places a small plastic bag of white powder close to Subrosa's face, and the disinterest in his voice turns my blood to ice. "Is that so, darling? Well, here's a little bonus then, for the pain, because I don't believe you."

He turns to Hatch. "Don't make a mess of her."

I scramble for cover in a dark recess of the hallway, flattening myself to oblivion as Byron exits and I almost lose the contents of my stomach. Too wise to scream, too disabled by the memory of my fear to intervene, sliding to the ground, legs like jelly, I am helpless as I stuff my fingers in my ears to drown out Subrosa's muffled cries of pain. And I piss myself.

⅄

I wait all night, hunkering down by the basement entrance at the back of the club, shrouded in Jesse's oversized parka, praying for Subrosa to appear, my heart sinking at the humiliation on her tear-stained face when she does emerge.

She sees me step out of the darkness, my arms ready to comfort her.

"Apparently, I've been a bad girl – though for fuck sake what, I haven't a baldy notion," she sniffs, and I know she is lying, her hands too trembling to light herself a cigarette. I take it from her, sniffing out the skag as I place it between her lips, flicking her lighter. How she pulls on that joint, a life saver, an anesthetiser, and still she leaves some for me. I take it.

And I walk her home, to her bedsit on the Norrier; to a once majestic tree-lined avenue that leads to the gates of the park. To a dingy basement door at the bottom of a neglected

Edwardian townhouse that gives no clue to the sublime wonder of her cave of colour. Her sparkling, mismatched, shabby chic oasis of calm.

"Why did he punish you? What's he looking for?" I ask. I know she's too valuable to him to take a beating for some missing drugs. There had to be more to it.

Her silence is not surprising, though her transformation is as the wig comes off, revealing her clean-shaven head. She leaves the small kitchenette and goes into a tiny bathroom, elbow-room only, returning with some facial wipes to clean her caked, tear-stained face. I watch her downgrade from bombshell to ordinary right before my eyes. But still, there is beauty there in the shadows and the stubble. She's comfortable enough with me to reveal herself, and I am flattered. I make myself useful, boiling the kettle for a cuppa and an early morning snack of cheese and bread, the only food I can find in the place.

"You first," she says, watching me, her long, false nail waving at me. "Why are you there, working for that monster?"

There's no butter, so I grate the cheese, squashing it onto a slice of stale white loaf bread before grilling it. I think of Jesse and how he loved this stodgy batch loaf, but I would never buy it for him. Fresh baked wholemeal, every day, no matter how much he protested.

I'm looking at Subrosa across the fold-up table covered in a rose-patterned vintage oil cloth. The cups, saucers and the plates are oddments, flea market bargains, and all so pretty. I like it here; it suits the new me. The comfort and the company overwhelms me and I can feel the lump in my throat, swelling, pushing.

I spill my guts, about Jesse, and Frankie, and suddenly her arms are around me, strong and muscled. Together, we cry, smoke hash and curl into each other on her tiny sofa bed, covered in a lime green, fake fur coat that she proudly tells me she'd bought for five euros at a car boot sale. We talk, long into the night. About other lives and other loves until exhaustion sends us into a stoned sleep.

It's well into the afternoon when we wake, and she tells me about her life before The White Lady, when she was Roddy, living a soul-destroying lie, with a civil service wage, a mortgage and a shit load of manic depression. Life was better now, she assured me – fun, despite the occasional thrashing on the whim of the boss. Besides, she had made up her mind now to get the fuck out.

She gives me something – a mobile phone she had been hiding under the floorboards beneath her bed.

"I won't be needing this, not any more. Watch the video on it," she says, "and be wise in what you do with it. It was sent to me by a boy I knew, and I believe, he was murdered because of it– not by Frazer, I can verify that – but, I believe, because of what he filmed."

"It's linked to *him* though? Byron? Is that why he had you—?"

"Interrogated?" she cuts in. "Yes. He's just as eager as the cops to know why Collins was killed. And by whom. I have my suspicions, but suspicions can get you killed."

She takes my hands in hers. "I have to get out of here. You understand? Frazer will be like a dog with a bone with this. Will you help me? Could I ... can I borrow some money? Enough to get me a plane ticket to Italy? I have some friends there. I could start afresh. In return, you could have this place, here, if you need it?"

A fair exchange, I think, though I will miss my new-found soul sister.

Of course I give her the money – all hail to the generosity of the credit union – and the taxi fare to get her to the airport in style.

When she is all packed up and gone, I watch the video on Subrosa's phone and I see through a dead kid's eyes. Another ghost to haunt my dreams. Only this one is speaking from beyond the grave, and what he is telling me is a game-changer.

⚔

I've known fear in all its guises. I've felt the sickening, overwhelming power of it. Still, I go back to the club, too far gone to stop now, biding my time for the right time.

And when my chance comes, I am ready.

He is alone and I remember clearly now how he likes to be alone, how he likes to watch the world he believes that he does not belong to, the world he looks down on. I make my move, appearing in front of him to place a drink on his table.

"Still like your brandy with cream liqueur?" I ask as he moves out of the shadow to glare at me.

Like clockwork, Mags is on me, sharp, acrylic fingernails digging into my arm while she apologises to the boss man. "I've been waiting to ask you about this one."

Her grasp draws blood, but I won't flinch for her. I keep my eyes on him, and he stares back at me, frowning.

I gesture at my surroundings. "A far cry from the flats now, isn't it?"

He says my name, *Elizabeth*, and Mags falls away and there is just me and him. I fight against the fear, the child junkie cowering inside me as he orders me to follow him to his office on the second floor. His womb-like construct, all curving shapes in purple and red, the club sounds oscillating through my limbs, pounding through the floor and walls as an inferior replacement for Miss Subrosa, coked-up and delicate, works the stage. I can see her on the giant plasma screen that takes up most of one wall of the office.

He still likes to watch.

"What do you think of her?" he asks, leaning back against his desk so that we are face to face.

I clutch the drinks tray close to my stomach, concentrating hard to stay standing on these jelly legs. He circles me silently. "A beauty? Though trouble is so often the same thing. How long it has been, Elizabeth, seventeen, eighteen years?"

I nod in silent agreement. I have to find a voice for him, a voice that won't betray me.

"You look good on it – stunning, as a matter of fact," he says. I guess I'm meant to be flattered by that. He moves in on me, taking his usual liberties to touch a strand of my hair, smoothing it back into place behind my ear. "You were always in a league of your own – a rare object, as I recall."

"Except I was too stupid back then to realise it," I reply. An object indeed! The tremor in my voice is real enough, though laden with a different emotion than the reverence he probably assumes it to be.

"Didn't I pay you enough attention? Is that why you ran?" he asks, attentive to my body language, to my heaving breath, the sweat on my upper lip.

I only told him half the story, of course. I left out the uglier bits. Need to know basis; never ask, never tell. He didn't deserve to know my journey outside of him – how I'd bought a ticket to the first destination that flashed at me from the train station departure board: Galway. The rhythm of the carriage gently rocking the fear away as I gained enough distance to exhale; to breathe into new beginnings.

"I wasn't very well, Byron, neither in mind nor body. I would have become a liability to you." Like so many before and after me, the broken kids who made their mistakes early on, kids like Frankie and Nellie, I remind myself, strengthening my resolve. But they're none of his business.

"You stole from me, Elizabeth. Why did you cross me like that?"

Miserable bastard, he probably knows the exact amount I took from him too.

"I always intended to pay you back, just as soon as I got myself well. I had to get away to do that. I was scared you'd reject me – that would have killed me – so I left before you got the chance to see how far I was gone."

His eyes are on me, those intense, hypnotic green eyes. I'm babbling now; he's not talking at all, the balance of power in his favour. Just the way I want it.

"Throughout our lives we meet the living angels," I say. "If we're lucky we recognise them before it's too late, before they disappear again. You were my first, Byron. You took me from the gutter. I couldn't ask that of you twice."

As he absorbs what I hope will be enough to stroke his ego, I think about the real first angel that helped me change my life. She appeared in the form of a social welfare officer. Linda was her name, and though she'd say she had just been doing her job, I know that when this skinny, pregnant, drug-infested teenager arrived on the other side of her desk, her compassion went beyond the call of duty. That night I had a clean warm room in a B&B in the town centre, and within a week, I was in receipt of an allowance that enabled me to go to a supermarket and buy the nourishment that my growing baby needed. And off her own bat, she checked in on me once in a while, helping me set up an appointment at the maternity hospital and making sure I disclosed my history of drug taking and sexual abuse, something I only managed to do once during the years that followed.

I healed fast, and all thanks to my son. His clean, pure essence flooding through me, purging the poison until I no longer craved it.

Linda taught me to cook cheap and nutritional meals, and I learned how to eat them – more than that, to enjoy them – and boy did I eat. By the time Jesse was due, I was plump and healthy and even my track marks had faded a little, though for years afterwards, I still covered my arms, even in summertime, and especially from my boy.

My boy.

As soon as Jesse was old enough to go to a crèche, I got a placement on a back-to-education scheme, though I'd never studied a day in my life. I was bright and learned quickly, and managed to finish the course that first year, studying at night with my child in my arms, still feeding from my breast. More importantly, I managed to stay off the drugs. There was no way I was hurting my little boy with that poison, or giving anyone a reason to take him away from me. I had found my bliss, my religion in his innocent eyes, and oh the joy of waking every morning to his special smell, his trusting little face, his tiny clinging fingers as he fed from me.

Getting off welfare was the next big step on the road to the life that I craved. There's a saying that what you need will come your way, and fuck, the joy and excitement when I got my first pay packet – clean money earned from clean living. It was an experience only surpassed months later when I got a letter telling me to collect the keys to my very first home – a council house that I could rent for a small sum from my wages. I didn't have a chair to sit on, but at least we were out of that one-room bedsit. I had windows that let in light and air, and a front door I could close behind me, locking out the hurt, the past. Nobody knew me or my history and I liked it that way, settling in well to a life of domesticity and simplicity, content to just be, to be with my son.

When I try to remember the finer details of those years now, they are something of a blur, lost forever to my distant past. But there was happiness as I spent my days balancing budgets and taking every opportunity for betterment; for him. To educate him was everything to me. To give him the tools to know himself with a confidence to make good decisions and to steer his own course, and to never know, nor make the mistakes that I had made. I learned to cope with the aloneness of being a single mother, a self-imposed celibate. In fact, I cherished it.

I was free of my past. I was free to be someone other than myself.

And I was never alone, with Jesse by my side. By the time he started school, I already knew he was a bright boy, growing fast and excelling at all his subjects and the sports he loved. All I had to do was make sure I could fund the activities he wanted to try – piano, then guitar, then swimming, and football, and rugby and on and on.

He got better looking every year too, and was popular with his friends, especially the girls. Only occasionally did I look into those gorgeous dark eyes and see something that made my insides tingle, not with joy, but with a cold dread.

I was so in love with him, it was easy to shake it off, to ignore my angst.

Nothing was too good for Jesse, and with my past well and truly buried, I could pretend it all away. My boy was my miracle. My boy was my saviour.

I had a plan. Saved money like a mad thing to get us back to Dublin. I was a woman now, with all those years between the old and the new, each one helping to fade the fear, the memories. Surely I was gone from that man's mind also?

All the hard work paid off when Jesse received his first-year bursary for academic achievement at the prestigious boarding school I had chosen for him. A day student, he would have everything I never had – the necessary preparation for the perfect life that lay ahead of him. The proceeding years brought crippling school fees, but luck was finally on my side. When I met my second angel: Luke. Saying his name should make my heart weep, but hearts can't always have their way.

"So you're here to pay me back, is that it?" Byron's tone is darker.

I'm looking at my hand, the one I mutilated with scalding water, a self-imposed punishment. I show it to him and watch as he recoils with the disgust that the sight of it evokes.

"I had a bit of trouble – a hitter – and I ran for my life. I thought of you."

I can see the slight throb in his neck, his misplaced revulsion at the idea that some man had inflicted such an injury on me. I hope that he is remembering, thinking of his mother. That he still holds onto that injustice. That I can work his only weakness to my advantage.

"I'm frightened, Byron. I need a place of safety, and to earn some money, but I understand if you want me to go."

Some things never change. I could see it in his eyes – the twisted fucker, with his shadows and demons, sympathizing with my helpless broken flesh – but I wasn't fooled. Byron Frazer's gaze upon me was filled with more than pity, it was calculating, it was seeing an opportunity. To own me. And to punish me for running out on him all those years ago.

I had pushed the right buttons, no matter how he tried to hide it.

"And what's in it for me, if I help you – again?" he asked.

I put the tray down – my shield is gone – and slowly get down on my knees. He takes hold of my hair as I open his trouser belt.

⚓

Bailey couldn't stop thinking about that woman, Beth Downes. He didn't seem to be able to shake her off. There was pity, for her loss. There was curiosity, for her links to that low-life. There was fascination, for her way of being.

On his fourth attempt to visit her, Beth finally opened the door and Bailey found himself lost for words at the transformation in her appearance. He'd seen plenty of people disintegrate after the loss of a loved one, but he had never witnessed anyone bounce back so soon. The vision before him did not look like a woman who was grieving. And it wasn't just her appearance that threw him.

"I've tried a couple of times to contact you, Miss Downes, concerning Frankie."

There it was, the dead space behind the eyes. She was looking at him, yet he knew she could barely see him. It irked him and the disappointment sat like a lead weight in his chest.

"What's to follow up, Detective Bailey, he's dead. Have you found his mother? Have you looked?"

Bailey raised his hands as if he was being held at gun-point, his body language working faster than his mouth. "We haven't been able to locate her. Is this a good time to talk to you about that? About Frankie? About his funeral arrangements?"

Now she was present; now he had her full attention.

"His funeral?" she whispered, stepping back from the door to let him in. "You mean he's still there, on a slab, all alone?"

She moved away from him into the sitting room, all those photographs still there, closing in on them. He watched her sink into a chair and perched opposite her, on the arm of her sofa, a futile attempt to feel less of an invader in her small, grief-riddled space.

"If no one claims him by tomorrow the state will have to bury him."

"I'll claim him!" she shouted. "Jesus, I should have known. I should've done it before now!"

Bailey tried to calm her. He could help.

"I don't need your help," she snapped. "I've bought a plot. My son is there. There's room for three, room for Frankie."

A silence hung in the air between them. Bailey wanted to stay, to ask questions, to break down her defences. Someone else was thinking of her, judging by the huge, wilting bouquet of flowers still in the cellophane wrap on the floor.

"How are *you* keeping, Beth?" The words just fell out of him and he cringed as she looked at him in surprise.

She turned her face away, her sideways mistrust. "So you're following up on Frankie's death, but not my son's?"

And there it was again, the reminder of his inadequacy. His failure to do his job.

"I'm not giving up on Jesse, I can promise you that," he said. He paused for a second, studying this intriguing woman. "I've heard a rumour that the Frazer girl, Rebecca, has been hospitalised. You know anything about that?"

"No, I hadn't heard," Beth said without taking her eyes off him. "Have you questioned her parents yet?"

Bailey wasn't about to go anywhere near the Frazer house – not yet, not until he had something concrete. He'd heard from an informant that Rebecca had suffered a breakdown, though he suspected it was drug related. Her father had spirited her off to some private rehab facility. Bailey would be treading very carefully around it. Couldn't afford to fuck that one up.

"Truthfully, Miss Downes, I don't have enough evidence to question either Rebecca or her parents. If you know something—"

"What I know won't help!" she snapped. "So if you're done now, please leave."

Bailey made his way to the front door. As Beth followed close behind, he braced himself for another verbal assault, but she surprised him with the softness in her voice.

"I'll let you know when I have Frankie's funeral arrangements sorted – if you like."

An affirmative nod was all he could manage before she closed the door on his retreat.

⚓

The boss man is probably watching me on the plasma screen as I continue to work the tables. I can imagine him zooming in on my face while I, smiling sweetly, deftly dodge yet another slimy grope. He'll like that, the fact that I am clean, but enough of a tease not to upset the clients.

Mags appears in her usual nasty guise to bark at me.

"The gentleman over there has requested that you attend to him. Be nice – he looks like money!"

I glance across to where she has gestured and freeze when I see Luke sitting alone at a table. Fuck! I simmer with rage that he's here; he scowls right back at me.

"Don't make a scene, Luke," I say, my lips clamped into a perfect smile.

But he grabs my arm. Stupid, stupid man!

"We're leaving!" he announces.

All I can think of is that Byron is watching this altercation from his office as I try to pull myself free of Luke's grasp, pleading with him to go away, to leave me alone. I swing round to sit on his lap, confusing him as I caress his chest, leaning in close to whisper in his ear: "I want you to get up and leave, right now. Don't make trouble for me. If you do this for me, I promise to come over to your place later and explain everything. Please."

He hesitates, but with my face fixed in that stupid fake smile, I beg again and again until, at last, he gets up angrily.

"I'll wait for you to finish your shift. It'll be your last one!"

And he is gone, much to my relief.

But I'm pissed off now and on edge. His visit is a real spanner in the works, and I grit my teeth. I'm so fucking mad at him. I'm still mad at closing time, that internal tremor there again. Knowing Byron will ask about him, and how I might explain it all as I try to concentrate on separating my tips from my daily float, careful not to make a mistake with his money as I wonder how I might get rid of Luke once and for all; the poor, kind, stupid bastard.

Before I can clear my head, Byron is there, behind me, standing very close, taking my hand, lifting it to his mouth and brushing his lips over the ugly, scarred flesh.

"You can stop running now, Elizabeth."

I clear my throat and swallow against the panic that might spew out from the back of my brain. "Thank you for the flowers." I manage. "You shouldn't have. Please don't spend your money on me. I'm really not worth it."

There was almost a smile until I uttered that last part, and I knew that I had vexed him.

"That guy – the one who was pestering you earlier – does he send you flowers? Your hitter?"

Jesus Christ. Panic engulfs me and I barely have time to take in the full ramifications of the conclusion he'd just jumped to. He flicks his green eyes away from me to a CCTV monitor behind the bar.

"It's a playback. The scum has been dealt a warning."

I try to stay calm and dispassionate as my heart thuds with every blow that Luke takes from Byron's scum bouncers. Crocodile tears, my mother used to call them when my skin and my pride stung, but now, I let them flow, cementing my belief that I am bad, that I am rotten to the core. Beyond redemption, I will do what it takes to save my sorry ass as I play this game for all it's worth.

"Maybe he'll leave me alone now," I cry out. "I can't defend myself any more. I'm so scared all the time. That's why I needed to find my way back to you, to where things are ordered and controlled. That's what I need now, Bryon. I have nowhere else to turn."

I wipe my face, my breathing shallow as I attempt to hide the real cause of my nausea, "Do you have any children?" I ask him, trembling in his scrutiny, and almost failing to hold my eyes on his as the CCTV screen goes black – and he is telling me that he has a daughter. Bullseye.

"Then maybe you can imagine the pain of losing her – like I lost my son. There's no heartache quite like it. It never leaves, even when I sleep." He's right there with me, no going back. "My boy died, and I'm afraid of my future without him."

Oscar performance, Lady! High five to your dear, disgusting, rotten self.

"I'm sorry to hear that, Elizabeth. I can only imagine the pain. A mother's love is like no other. The love of the helpless." He touches my face, liberties taken once again. "My boys will take you home. Pack your stuff up. I'll sort out a place for you to stay tomorrow."

Trembling, my heart racing so painfully that I wonder if he can hear it, I squeeze my eyes shut and take a deep breath. Another step closer to ending this hell. Together we leave the club, Wally and Hatch appearing by his side, sharing some private joke between them, probably at Luke's expense, his blood still staining their knuckles. Byron opens the car door and ushers me inside. I have to be so careful now. I hesitate.

"Your guys scare me," I say and refuse to move. Where the strength to keep playing comes from, I don't know, but I am resolved. "And I don't want to go home, with all its reminders. I want to be with you."

When he doesn't respond, I start to back away, fragile, helpless little me, the grieving mother, and I can see that he's intrigued, and amused. Behind him, his thugs smirk and suddenly he's irritated by them, dismissing them: *Get the fuck out of here.*

"Elizabeth!"

I want to run, to change my mind, but I can't. "I've had enough of being afraid, Byron. I'd rather float down the river than keep living like this – in fear, in grief – and have no one to turn to."

The gospel truth of that comes easy, and he's blocking my path, sucked in as I blabber on about how he might be interested to see where I've been hiding. He can hardly believe it when I remind him of where we first did it.

"Do you remember, Byron? We have our ghosts, don't we? We have our ghosts back there in the blocks. You and I – our history in that tomb."

His expression clouds and I know that he's back there, but he says nothing.

"But if you can't help me, with all of our shared history, I guess I'll have to take my chances on the streets."

I am fucking petrified by the shadow that falls across his gaze and suddenly he is grabbing at me, frisking my body roughly, hands and fingers unsparing. He can't be too careful. I might be concealing something from him. When he's done he pushes me into the passenger seat of the car. Sure, we'll take a trip down memory lane: *Why the fuck not.*

I've won the first round, but there are many still to come, and I'm not sure that I'm strong enough, reality biting hard as he produces a small white pellet from his pocket and waves it in my face.

I summon a smile. "Can we save that for later," I say sweetly.

But his mouth is hard now. "No honey, not later – now."

He breaks the capsule open, taps the white powder on to the back of his hand and sticks it under my nose.

"It was always part of your charm," he says, "the way you used to sizzle."

It's another test, and if I fail I'll be floating down that river after all. I take his hand and slowly draw his poison into my nostrils.

⟡

Bailey entered the station and went straight to the desk sergeant, who pointed towards Luke, slumped in the waiting area, black and blue.

As the pieces of the puzzle spill from him, all Bailey can think of is that petite grieving lady and her golden eyes, her heartache and ... what the fuck was she up to!

Exhausted and resigned, Luke rolled a piece of crumpled paper between his fingers. "I asked her once why she never looked at me, but she didn't understand the question. Do you know what I mean, Detective?"

Bailey, uncomfortable with the question, lowered his eyes as if to examine his shoes.

"It is the look from the woman you desire, that ache of want - a look that I now know she is incapable of giving, to me, to anyone."

Luke offered the crumpled piece of wallpaper to Bailey. On the back of it, he could just about decipher the words that Frankie had scribbled there. Luke got up to leave, mumbling the words as he went, "His death was her death, and she is running towards it."

I had cleaned it up as best I could, though I could still smell and feel him there – my ghost boy. Byron looks so out of place in Frankie's filthy, sparse flat, yet he was doing his best to fit right in. I've broken out in a sweat, and I can't stop the inner tremors, the rush of that poison in my veins. But I can still pretend to be flirtatious. I hold it together long enough to remove my coat and open the bottles of brandy and cream liqueur that I had placed on the window sill before starting work earlier. I pour him a large glass, swirling the mixture before offering it to him. He can't believe that I am hiding out in this shithole, but I don't want him to talk.

Talking is not what we've come here for.

I put my hands on his shoulders and push him gently down on to a kitchen chair. I straddle his lap, my movements deliberate so I don't lose it, but my lips quiver and I am flushed and sweating from that old friend in my veins. I am fighting though, still fighting.

He pushes me to the floor, so much stronger than I, and it's all I can do to stop myself from vomiting as he rips open my clothes. He fucks me right there on the dirty floor, and just like I used to, I go outside myself. I remember a story that Frankie had told me about him, The Poet. How during his twelve-year incarceration he had been famous for spending his nights alone in his cell reading from a book, the poetry by Lord Byron. A gift he had given to his mother for her birthday not long before her death. Barely literate as a child, he had been attracted by the bright golden letters on the spine and, recognising his own name, had stolen the book from a street market stall, scrawling a love message to his ma on the imprint page.

I could imagine her now, reading to him at night, the meanings alien to him, but the sound of her soothing voice lulling him to sleep. And I cry inside, the great big hollow inside me still yearning for my Jesse.

When he's done, I'm surprised how clean and quick it all is. Maybe he has mellowed with age, his stamina failing. Maybe this will be easier than I thought.

He kisses my neck and I'm surprised by the tenderness of his touch.

"Why do men become destroyers?" I ask.

"Are women not destroyers too?" he replies, lifting me gently to my feet.

"Not in the pursuit of power," I say. "But yeah, I guess they can be."

Just when I thought he had changed his sadistic habits, Byron grabs my thigh, his fingers digging so hard into my flesh that I almost scream out in agony. He jerks my head back and I try to resist. The walls are closing in on me. I beg him to give me a minute, but he's already between my legs. A rage surges through me from god knows where and I shove him, punching his hands away, forcing him off me just long enough for me to get to the bedroom.

"I said – give me a minute!"

Perhaps he is amused at my attempt for dominance, all part of the game, and he allows me a momentary respite before he follows me, hovering in the doorway, knocking back another large drink, sussing out the situation. In the glow of candlelight, every fucking thing can look good. Every fucking thing can look romantic. I am completely naked now, a small leather whip in my hand, pinched from Miss Subrosa's dressing room after she had gone.

At once terrified and buzzed up; his very own white lady.

Byron lets me undress him and I tease him with the whip, running it along his thighs. He moans with anticipated pleasure, tries to take the whip from me. I'm not giving it up yet. I slap him just hard enough to surprise him with my aggression, but he inevitably wins as he roughs me up, smacking me as he rolls me on to my stomach. I stare at the pattern on the wallpaper, the faded kingfishers coming in and out of focus until all is black and I succumb to the curtain of red blood behind my closed lids.

But I hear him, Frankie, calling out to me: *Lady, Lady*, and I fight back to consciousness, and when the boss man is done a second time, I draw every ounce of strength left in me to take advantage of his fucking little death. I want to claw his eyes out, puke all over his rotten face, but from somewhere, maybe from that white poison, I draw the fire to play on, taking advantage of that *sizzle* to drive him to the edge with my lips, my breasts, my fingers as he moans and claws at me. I have no time to waste, reaching across his almost spent body to retrieve the velvet ties I had earlier stuffed under the mattress. He makes a half-hearted effort to take them from me, but I am carrying on, tying his right wrist to the bedpost, all the while kissing him gently as I do the same with his left. My breathing is so painful now that I think I might have a heart attack as I fake on, sliding down, my hot breath on his skin, and he lies in surrender and anticipation as I tie each ankle to the bedposts.

I take a moment to slow my breath, counting five in, ten out. My heart rate goes down and I slip off the bed to turn on the light. Byron is spreadeagled, out cold. Finally, the spiked brandy kicking in. I prod and shake him and still he doesn't waken. But I am not done yet, my body repulsed and shivering, pulling my coat over it, vulnerability all wrapped up once more as I spit on the floor and wipe my mouth clean with my sleeve.

Rifling through his pockets, my inner junkie child moves deftly. I find his mobile phone, turn off the power and place it back in his pocket after wiping it clean of my prints. I take his pack of cigarettes and check his other pocket. My heart leaps when I find a small handgun, and

I thank my lucky angels that I hadn't known it was there before. I study it carefully, wondering if he has ever used it, if it has maimed or killed someone, and I put it carefully in my coat pocket.

What I'll do with it I'll figure out later as I kneel down to reach under the bed for the heavy-duty rolls of duct tape I had stashed there earlier. The sound of it ripping from the sticky roll, flesh from bone, gives me an adrenaline rush, flushing my skin with heat and giving a kick to my cold, dead heart.

⚔

How I relish the moment when the curtains are pulled back violently to cast a harsh light on that face. I sit watching him as he opens his eyes, squirming to free his arms, his legs, his own belt strapped to the headboard, firm and tight around his neck. He squints painfully as I surely come into focus, straddled across a chair at the end of the bed.

His voice is hoarse. "Playtime is over now, honey, untie me."

I watch his growing panic as I fail to follow orders, his struggle causing him to gag every time he tries to raise his head. I should really advise him to be still, tell him he'll only make it worse for himself. But I don't. I take one of his cigarettes and light up.

"Your head must hurt," I say, "but it's just the shit load of sleeping pills I put in your drink. Same ones the doctor gave me to help me through my bereavement."

Byron's humiliation turns to confusion as I reach closer, holding the cigarette inches from his face. "Think it's your turn now, to sizzle."

I point at the ceiling and hear a sharp intake of breath as Byron sees the blown-up photograph taped to the ceiling above him. Jesse and his beloved daughter.

"Makes it easier for me to understand his obsession with her," I say. "Such a beautiful girl with so much potential, yet she screws around, takes affection anywhere she can get it, destroys everything she touches. She didn't lick that off the ground, now did she?"

The boss man's eyes flick from my boy to Rebecca and I see the moment when the penny drops.

"I heard it said somewhere that boys who live alone with their mothers have a special face. And do you see those eyes, Byron? Recognise your own eyes? I wish you could hear it like I still hear it – my boy's pleading voice when all is dark and quiet and he whispers to me from the white noise. And that last bitter fight, him spitting still with the residue of fury from the one before it, when I tore into him, a rage I never knew I had in me. A rage he never knew I had in me. And later, when he tried to apologize in his awkward, half-hearted way, I saw right through him. And he saw right through me, bullseye in the heart with his best shot; the Daddy question. Of course I couldn't tell him about you, so I did the only thing I could – I ran from his frustrated anger and hid in the bathroom, my hands over my ears as my son screamed insults at me from the other side of the door. And then my boy was dead, on a dirty floor while I sat alone, miserable and slumped across my kitchen table, watching the clock, waiting to hear his key in the door, his return to me. You know what killed him? Our boy? I'll tell you what killed him. Her. That daughter of yours, all pouty smiles and poison. And he's not her only victim. I heard she cracked up. Is that true, Byron?"

"You better untie me, you crazy fucking bitch!" he screams.

"You better pay attention, you miserable motherfucker!" I scream back, pulling the gun from my pocket and shoving it in his face. "And I won't be starting with your fingers!"

My fear has subsided, gone to ground as I move my chair closer to the bed.

"I bet your poor dead mother would be disgusted to know the terrible example you've set for your precious Rebecca. Do you know what her favourite tipples are? Amphetamines, the ones you have all dressed up as little green sweets, and maybe some china white, charlie, snow, blow, or whatever it is you lot like to call it these days. The same stuff you used to feed me, until I progressed to the heroin. Still like them young, Byron? Young like I was back then? Guess that would make you a fucking pervert."

I touch the skin on the back of my hand, trace the mound of scalded tissue, and feel every other scar I've earned, the most vile ones incubated within.

"Remember once you punished me – or rather you got your scumbag goon-of-the-day to do it? I can't even remember now what it was for, but I remember the pain. All your sanctimonious bullshit about not hitting women, not beating them like your mother had been beaten – it's okay as long as someone else does it for you though, right? You cowardly bastard!"

I hold the lit cigarette close to his eye, so close, the ash falls on to his cheek.

"Get the fuck away from me!"

He can scream all he likes, I tell him; no one can hear him. Even if they do, people don't interfere in domestics, now do they?

I toss back my hair and tut-tut, just like I used to do when Jesse was naughty. The glowing ash is burning down, closer, closer to the white of his eye. It's tempting, but the last thing I want is for Byron to die blind – at least not before his gets to see my second surprise. To his temporary relief, I pull the cigarette away and stamp it out on the floor. I can see the fear in his eyes as I place the gun against his forehead.

I think about that fear in Frankie and Subrosa and it makes my fucking blood boil.

"How many lives have you destroyed, Byron? Apart from your Daddy's? But he doesn't really count now, does he? He was a hitter. Dirty rotten scum."

I remove the gun. The barrel leaves a circular impression on his skin, a tiny halo branded on the forehead of the devil.

"Oh, I know that other people do your dirty work, but you still like to watch, don't you?"

He follows me around the room with his confused, terrified eyes, positively bulging from their sockets when I slowly roll down one stocking, then the other.

"You remember Frankie, don't you? Just a kid he was, and a runner, just like me. Easy prey for you, just like I was."

I yank his head up by the hair, stuff the stocking into his mouth and let go.

"And that Collins kid. Didn't know him myself, though a friend of mine told me all about him."

I've been holding on to the mobile phone that Subrosa had given me. I've played the video over and over. At first, I didn't really know what the hell I was witnessing, but when I realised it was his precious Rebecca hanging from those hooks, spilling her own blood for some kind of twisted release, swaying in ecstasy as that poor boy, Collins, secretly filmed her, I knew I could win.

"You know what she did, your little precious? She gouged out the eyes of a boy for the sin of filming her. You knew about Collin's death, didn't you? A real conundrum for you, especially with the rumours that she was hanging out with your daughter. Bet she denied any knowledge of him, thinking she had gotten rid of the evidence. But she hadn't planned on him sending the link to a friend of ours before she got her murderous claws into him."

Byron is beyond terror now, his breathing laboured, his eyes popping.

"You spawned quite a little devil in that one, didn't you? And you know all about retribution?" I am whispering now, close to his ear, "As you said yourself, women can be destroyers."

I hold the phone up close to his face and play the video for him. Rebecca Frazer, hanging from meat hooks, the stoned, swaying marionette, her white skin punctured with holes, a zoomed in shot of her face revealing her love of pain, just like Daddy.

I kiss the fucker's cheek and a low howl gurgles from him before I close the curtains again, relight the candle and pick up the gun.

"When you knew me back then, Byron, when I was a naïve strung out little kid, did you ever think I'd be capable of destroying you?"

His stifled gasps fill the room.

"I've done a lot of thinking about it, how it would feel taking your life from you. How it would sound, your last breath."

I put a pillow over his face and press the gun into it. His body bucks and strains, his pleas are muffled. I make a sound of a gunshot: *bang*.

"Refrain from belligerence," I whisper, snatching the pillow away. "But you know, don't you, Byron? You know."

I watch his chest heave in and out, turning concave as he struggles for air.

"You know you can never destroy what is already dead."

I tighten the belt a notch around his neck and sit back in the chair.

"They say that at the end, your life flashes before you – all the people you've known, all the people you've hurt, the ones you've loved. Your mother, Byron – can you see her yet? How come you didn't learn anything righteous from her murder? You've clearly felt that pain, that loss." Byron's chest heaves as he struggles to take shallow breaths. As his body jerks, trying to ease the strain on the belt, I'm looking off to a corner in the room, seeing my ghost child there, slumped, his beautiful eyes, hollow sockets, watching me as Frankie's soulful face transforms to Jesse's.

"Mothers get a hard time, don't they? Trying to raise their boys right. Sometimes, though, their boys disappoint them, break their hearts. And mothers can't compete with their addictions."

I wait and watch as death creeps slowly in to choke the life from him. As Byron Frazer strangles himself. I suspect he suffers a massive heart attack, but I couldn't be sure. I'm not in any hurry, so I don't move until his body finally stops jerking and is still.

The Poet, still and dead. And I wait until it is dark once more, and only then, I carefully gather everything I have brought with me – even the velvet ties and the photograph on the ceiling – and I gently cut away the duct-tape from his limp wrists and ankles, picking up the gun to polish away my fingerprints and replace it in his jacket pocket.

I leave him there, laid out in all his naked glory, with only the belt secured around his neck, and gathering all my stuff, and Frankie's, I throw everything into a plastic bag, except for one thing. The phone, with the video of the swaying marionette, which I place in Bryon's hand, and I never look back as the sound of my exit echoes through that desolate tomb of misery.

When I kissed Jesse goodbye in the morgue that night, they hadn't even wiped away the blood that had pumped from his nose. I like to think they were too busy trying to revive him, but in my heart I know that they never even got that far. People looked at me, sideways glances. *She's a strange one, she is. Why isn't she crying?* But they couldn't hear the screaming, the scratching inside my veins.

Jesse was twenty-two inches long when he was born, and weighed ten pounds, two ounces. His birth was my rebirth. I asked the universe for him to be healthy, and I thought the universe had answered my prayers. But nothing could change the fact that he had our blood in his veins.

I accept my fate. His death is my death and I am running towards it, and will keep running. But I have purpose now, with my different face. I am stronger. And I am not finished.

⅄

Eric Bailey sits in his parked car with the lights out, engine off, concealed in the shadows of the derelict apartment blocks. His gaze is focused on one window half way up one of the towers, a small light flickering through the gap of a torn curtain, a wake being held in Frankie's tomb.

He does not move as he listens to the echo of stiletto heels running through the courtyard, away from the desolate buildings, and watches her shadow melt into the black of the starless night.

In time, he will get out of the car. In time, he will investigate the source of that small flickering light, his movements measured as he returns to that hovel where Frankie Harte still whispers from the walls. Where he will find the still warm body of Byron Frazer hissing and expelling gases, still clutching that phone. Bailey will watch the video, just once, before the battery dies, and he will know that this festering legacy, much like the stench that emanates from its dead patriarch, will linger on; a murderous marionette.

ACKNOWLEDGEMENTS

So many people to thank, and my sincere apologies if I've forgotten anyone! First off, as this story originally came to me as an idea for a screenplay, I would like to thank the original members of *The Kildare Screenwriters Group* for the initial sparks of encouragement to keep going with it. Also from the film world, deepest appreciation to *Michael Kinirons, Dermot Tynan*, and *Ozzy* and *Gabriel Villazon*. To the late *Gill Dennis* – my eternal gratitude for the confidence instilled in me through his kindness and support. I would like to thank *The Attic Studio Actors* for the public script reading that almost scared me to death, but ultimately was hugely helpful and inspiring: *Geraldine McAlinden, Joe McKinney, Sinead Monaghan, Michael Bates, Blayne Kelly, Laura Way* and *Melissa Nolan* – your collective feedback was invaluable, then and now. To *The Writers Guild of Ireland* and the amazing group of writer friends I found there: for the readings, the feedback and the laughter! BIG THANKS! To my wonderful soul friend, *Julie Luttrell*. To my editor, *Averill Buchanan*, for putting some manners on my scribblings. To the amazing *Lindsay J. Sedgwick* for her support through the blood, sweat and tears proceedings, and to the lovely *Celine Broughal* for the constant encouragement. Special thanks to *Mike Murray* (www.13thdoor.net) for the beautiful cover design, and to actress and producer, *Sinead O'Riordan* (www.sineadoriordan. com) and photographer, *Anita Kulon* (www.facebook.com/ Anita-Kulon-Photography) for permission to use the stunning image. To my readers: what good is a storyteller without you? And it goes without saying: to the most patient man on the planet, my better half, Errol, as always.

About the Author

Caroline E. Farrell is a writer and filmmaker from Dublin, Ireland, and is the author of the supernatural novel and screenplay ARKYNE, STORY OF A VAMPIRE. Caroline has also written several award-winning feature length and short screenplays and has co-produced two short films of her work, ADAM [2013] and the multi-award winning IN RIBBONS [2015].

Contact Caroline

Website: https://carolinefarrellwriter.com/

Facebook: https://www.facebook.com/
CarolineFarrellScreenwriter/

Twitter @CarolineAuthor

Instagram: https://www.instagram.com/carolineefarrell/

Made in the USA
Columbia, SC
12 April 2017